A Basket of Roses

A Basket of Roses

Angela Elwell Hunt

Tyndale House Publishers, Inc.
Wheaton, Illinois

Library of Congress Catalog Card Number 90-71570
ISBN 0-8423-0463-0
Printed in the United States of America

99 98 97 96 95 94 93 92 91
9   8   7   6   5   4   3   2   1

Important People in My Life, by Cassie Perkins

1. Glen Perkins, my dad. ♥♥♥♥♥.
   A systems analyst at Kennedy Space Center, and
   my favorite singer. Handsome, even if balding.
   Now separated from my mom and living in a
   condo. Not dating anyone now. Sometimes I
   wonder if he gets lonely, but he always seems to
   be working.
2. Claire Perkins, my mom. ♥♥♥♥♥.
   An interior decorator at home. When Dad left
   she cried a lot, and I hated it. Now she's not
   crying because she's got a rich boyfriend, Tom
   Harris. But I hate him worse than her crying.
3. Max Brian Perkins, my brother. ♥♥♥♥♥!
   Max lives with Dad in the condo. Now Max is
   not only cute and genius-smart, but he's rich,
   too! He sold his algae dog food to a company for
   twenty thousand dollars! That will buy him a lot
   of Twinkies!
4. Suki Buki Perkins, my Chinese pug. ♥♥♥♥♥♥♥!
   'Nuff said.
5. Andrea Milford, my best friend. ♥♥♥♥.
   We've had our ups and downs as friends, but I
   guess we'll be friends forever.
6. Chip McKinnon, the cutest guy I know ♥♥♥♥♥.
   Through thick and thin, Chip's been one of my
   best friends.
7. Tom Harris, the rich lawyer Mom's been dating.
   Mom met him at a meeting for the School for

the Performing Arts, so I guess it's sort of my fault. But I'd do *anything* to break them up.

8. Nick Harris, Tom Harris's son. ♥♥.
I liked him for a while because he's cute and nice, or so I thought. Now I think he's a spoiled rich kid. If Andrea wants him (and she does, I think), she can have him!

9. Jacob Benton, or Uncle Jacob. ♥♥♥.
Nick's uncle and the "housewife" of the Harris house. But I'd never say that to his face. He'd growl at me. He's a columnist for the paper, too, and a pretty good writer. I like him. I wish Mom would go out with him!

10. Shalisa McRay, this too-good-to-be-true girl I met at the School for the Performing Arts, or the Spa, as she calls it. ♥♥
She's friendly, but she's not the kind I'd call on the phone just to talk. Know what I mean?

Bells don't ring in this school. They hum. Delicately. A quiet little *hmmm* on about a B flat. Back at old Astronaut Junior High, bells didn't hum; they clanged. It was the only way they could be heard above the noise of thirty or so kids piled into a classroom.

But here at the School for the Performing Arts, or the Spa, as we call it, there are only ten kids per class, and the floors are all carpeted so any noise is muffled. The teachers are soft-spoken people who wear blazers with fancy crests embroidered on their breast pockets, and even the students are relatively quiet. I've never seen such well-mannered people.

After the humming of the bell, Shalisa McRay looked over at me. "So, Cassie, how did you like your first week of school here?" she asked, smiling her perfect smile.

I shrugged. "Fine. I didn't get lost, nobody picked on me, and I'm not flunking out yet."

Shalisa shook her head. "Really, Cassie, you come up with the oddest things! Whoever would pick on you?"

I only said those things because my best friend, Andrea Milford, had stayed over last weekend before *her* first day of school at Astronaut High. "It'll be terrible without you, Cassie," she had moaned. "I'll get lost in that big old school, and I've heard that seniors love to pick on freshmen. And they say the teachers are hard and—" She broke into tears. "I've never gone to school without you!"

She was right; we've gone to school together since kindergarten. All the excitement I had felt about getting a scholarship to attend the Spa had drained away as Andrea cried into my favorite stuffed animal, Mr. Willie; but not even Mr. Willie's bulging eyes or green frog legs could make Andrea feel better.

"You'll be fine." I tried to soothe her. "Remember, you always said high school would be fun because there are more hunks per square foot."

Andrea wiped her eyes and looked up. "That's right, isn't it? And since you'll be away at that snobby school, maybe Chip will need some company."

I shook my finger at her and smiled. "You stay

away from Chip, you hear? You can be friends only."

"OK." Andrea smiled and flashed her dimple. "I'll expand my horizons, I promise." She gave Mr. Willie another hug and looked over at me. "But you're so lucky, Cassie Perkins."

I didn't really feel lucky. Sure, it was great that I had won the Constance Hamilton Scholarship so I could attend the Spa for four years. And sure, for two or three weeks after hearing the news I had walked around in a happy daze. But school was school, and I wasn't sure I liked school at the Spa better than at Astronaut High with my friends. The work here was harder, the books were thicker, and everyone took everything so seriously! Max, my brainy little brother, would have loved it. But I wanted to sing, not study Greek tragedies!

Fortunately, after the humming of the last bell, school is over and the real fun begins. At two o'clock I have voice lessons with Mrs. Blackwelder, and at two-thirty, studio dance with Mr. Levy. I have my own personal practice room reserved from three until three-thirty, and I can even ask one of the kids on a work-study scholarship to be my personal accompanist while I'm rehearsing. It's unbelievable, and I love it.

Best of all, students at the Spa produce and

sing in three musicals each year. Monday afternoon Miss Cason, the theater director, will tell us about the musical we're performing in November. Auditions will begin next week, with rehearsals soon after. If I'm lucky enough to get a part, I'll be staying at school in rehearsals every day from three-thirty until five. If I don't get a part, I'll be painting sets or something, but that's part of the arrangement. Everybody does something, and nobody is a star all the time.

Except maybe Shalisa. I met Shalisa at the orientation meeting during the summer and found out that her grandmother is on the board of directors. I'm not saying she doesn't deserve the parts she gets—because Shalisa is a really good singer—but Shalisa seemed to get first pick when it came to choosing her voice teacher and her accompanist. I figured I'd just have to live with it until I proved myself.

Mrs. Blackwelder gave me a new piece of music today, a German song that I'm supposed to sing—in German, of course. "Don't even think about singing words this week," she said. "Just learn the melody on an 'ah,' and we'll learn the German next week, OK?" She played the song for me, stumbling as she went (piano was obviously not her strong point), and guided me over the rough spots with her strong soprano voice.

When I first started voice lessons with Mrs. Blackwelder, I had no idea what she was talking about most of the time. "Sing covered tones, not through the nose," she told me, "but in your head."

Covered tones? Sing in my head? I tried to do what she said, but she closed her eyes, grunted, and gave her head a little shake. "Like this," she commanded, and sang a scale in her rich voice that sounded like an opera singer's.

"Now you," she said, so I opened my mouth and imitated an opera singer. Max would have been on the floor laughing at me, but Mrs. Blackwelder looked satisfied. "Very good," she said, nodding. "Much improved."

Next was studio dance, which was a welcome break. Studio dance isn't what you see on American Bandstand. It's very regimented. We line up in straight lines and learn steps so that when Mr. Levy calls out "Grapevine for eight," we know that we're going to do that "step-back, step-over" routine that I think of as "one, two, a-three, four, five, a-six, seven, eight." It's fun, except when you make a mistake. Then lean and mean Mr. Levy casts his eagle eye your way, and you wish the floor would swallow you whole.

Shalisa, of course, is as graceful as a scarf billowing in the breeze. She knows all the moves by heart and smiles and watches her hand or the air or anything except her feet. I spend most of my time watching my neighbor's feet, so I don't trip and get both of us in trouble. Shalisa is the willowy reed bending in the wind; I'm the dumpy little frog that keeps squatting and jumping, trying to keep up.

After dance, I wiped my sweaty neck with a towel from my locker and hurried to my practice room. I didn't feel much like practicing, so I just sat on the piano bench and rested my arms and head against the piano. One week of school done; only thirty-five more to go. Those productions had better be spectacular because they were the brightest spots in my future. I only hoped I could get a good part.

I caught a city bus for a ride home. Mom had been really busy with her interior decorating business lately since her boyfriend, Tom Harris, gave her a contract to redecorate his law offices. I didn't really like Tom Harris, but I was glad Mom was busy with a job. For a few months after my dad moved out, Mom wallowed in a pity party every day, moaning about money, marriage, and missing Max. (Max, my genius brother, lives with Dad in a condo on the beach.) Then Tom Harris came along, and Mom stopped moaning and started smiling again.

Now, if only Tom Harris would leave, Mom and I could get back to normal.

Mom was home and even cheerier than usual. "Hi, honey," she called from the kitchen when I came in. "How was school today?"

"Fine," I answered, looking around for my welcoming committee of one. Sure enough, here came the wonder dog: my pug, Suki. Eight years old and pudgy, she clicked her nails across the floor as she hustled toward me. You may not believe me, but pugs can smile. Suki smiles most of the time, especially when I come home. It's great.

I stooped down to pet Suki. "What's up?" I called to Mom, who hardly ever worked in the kitchen.

"I picked up some Twinkies for Max." Mom came around the corner carrying a bulging grocery bag. "Your father hasn't been getting Max's Twinkies, and I promised Max I'd send some with you today. Just make sure he doesn't eat them all at once, OK?"

I groaned. I'd forgotten this was my weekend to stay with Dad and Max at the condo. I'd had a big week at school, and I was pooped. "Do I have to go?" I tried to look tired and a little sick. "I've had a busy week."

Mom wasn't about to be swayed. "We've all had a busy week. It's your weekend with your father, and I won't let him say I kept you away. You've got to go."

I sighed. Mom probably had plans with Tom—that's why she wanted me out of the way.

"Do you have a date?"

"Nothing special." Mom shrugged. "Tom invited me over for dinner. Uncle Jacob is making his famous London broil tonight." She gave me a curious little smile. "Do you want me to tell Nick hello for you?"

"No, Mom, that's all over."

"I thought you liked him."

"As a person, yes. As a boyfriend, well—" I had to be honest. "I used to like Nick, but I woke up and realized he's nothing special."

"OK, but I think he's a nice boy." Mom tied the plastic handles of the grocery bag into a neat little knot. "Just remember to give these to Max, OK?"

I grunted in response and carried my books to my room, with Suki trotting right behind.

2

Dad honked the horn instead of coming to the door to get me. That was unusual, but maybe he was in a hurry. "Bye, Mom," I called, gathering my overnight bag, my music, and Max's Twinkies. "See you Sunday night."

Bertha, Dad's blue sedan, was shinier than usual. "What's up?" I asked, piling into the car and tossing the grocery bag to Max. "Why did you give Bertha Blue a shine?"

"It's all part of the plan, Gypsy Girl," Dad said, using his pet name for me. He grinned at me in the rearview mirror. "You'll see tomorrow."

Max looked at me and raised his eyebrow. He obviously knew something but couldn't say. I'd just have to wait until I caught Max alone. Knowing Dad, he could have planned anything. He's a systems analyst at Kennedy Space Center— very smart, and very creative.

"So how was your first week of eighth grade, kiddo?" I asked Max. "Did any of the older kids pick on you?"

"No," Max said, shaking his head. "But my teachers said I should move up another grade. They want to send me to Astronaut High, but I want to talk to Mom first."

"A ten-year-old in ninth grade?" I shook my head. Max would be in the same grade as me, but he'd be at Astronaut High, with Chip and Andrea, my friends. I didn't doubt that he was smart enough, but it was hard to imagine him playing basketball with high school seniors. Max was only four foot eight.

"You don't have to talk to your mother, Son," Dad interrupted, glancing over at Max. "I'm your custodial parent, and if you want to go to Astronaut, it's fine with me."

"I'd still like to talk to Mom," Max said, shifting uneasily in his seat. "Don't take it personally, Dad."

Dad frowned, and Max and I stared out the windows. Ever since Dad had left, we often fell into these contests of Dad against Mom, or Mom spying on Dad, or both of them playing twenty questions about the other one. It was no fun at all.

I tried to change the subject. "What's the big plan for tomorrow, Dad? Are we going sailing?

16

To Kennedy Space Center? Is there a launch tomorrow?"

"Tomorrow is September 8," Dad said slowly. "And we're going out to commemorate the day."

September 8? I searched every brain cell to come up with some meaning for September 8 but couldn't think of anything. Why was it a day to commemorate instead of celebrate? Dad didn't offer any new information, and Max was busy scribbling on a piece of paper in his lap.

After a minute, Max casually tossed the paper over the seat to me. I picked it up and read: *September 8—six months are up. The divorce is final tomorrow.*

It seemed hard to believe, and yet it wasn't. After all, Dad and Mom had been living apart for more than six months. Max and I had been living apart, too—Max with Dad, me with Mom. Dad had dated, and Mom had dated, and we had done everything divorced families are supposed to do. We fought, we got support checks, we cried, we yelled, our parents talked to lawyers, and Max and I even had to tell a judge we thought it was OK that Max should live with Dad and I should live with Mom.

Of course, it wasn't really OK. It was just our only choice. All along, we hadn't been really divorced, just separated. Until now. Now it was really going to happen.

When we got to Dad's place, he went for his

usual after-work walk on the beach, and Max and I sat at the kitchen table. "Just think," I said, "after tomorrow, Mom and Dad won't be married anymore. You'll live with Dad, and I'll live with Mom, and we won't be a family anymore." I picked up a pen and began to doodle on a napkin. "I have this funny feeling I should change my name or something."

"Why?" Max asked. He grinned. "What's wrong with Cassiopeia Priscilla Perkins?"

I cringed. I always do when I hear my mouthful of a name. "Dad was the one who named me after a constellation," I said with a shrug. "So shouldn't I drop that name and go by Priscilla? That was Mom's choice."

Max's hands flew out in frustration. "Honestly, Cassie, can't you see that you're not the one who's changing here? You're not divorced, your parents are. You won't change, at least not legally. You are still the daughter of Claire and Glen Perkins, whether they're married or not. Besides," he said, leaning toward me, "if you go by *Priscilla,* you know what people will call you? Prissy."

For some reason I thought of Shalisa, who was as prissy as a girl could be. "No," I said, shaking my head. "Never. All I've ever wanted is a normal name and a normal family."

"According to statistics, you have a normal family," Max said. "There are two children,

18

two parents, a dog, and two cars. That's so normal, it's boring. Your parents just don't live together anymore, that's all. They are divorced, and divorce is not abnormal." He shrugged his shoulder. "At least, not anymore."

I knew Max was right, but I couldn't help feeling that tomorrow would change things drastically. I put my head down on the table. "Why didn't they name you after a constellation? Or a rocket? Why didn't they name you Gemini or Apollo Perkins?"

Max smiled and his eyes shone with mischief. "I'd rather be Hercules," he said, flexing his skinny ten-year-old arm. "I could take on all those big guys in gym class with no problem."

The next morning Dad told us to get dressed because we were going out. I looked up at Max, who was eating his Wheaties and Twinkies. Max shook his head and kept eating.

"Where are we going, Dad?" I called. "How should I dress?"

"Casual," Dad called from his room. "We're going to Hammer Auto. Old Bertha Blue is going for her last ride with the Perkins family."

The Perkins family—what there was of it— piled into Dad's blue car and drove to Hammer Auto. Dad had given Bertha one last polish, I realized, so she would look good when he traded her in. Max and I settled back into some uncomfortable vinyl-covered chairs while Dad and a salesman roamed through the parking lot looking at new cars.

"What kind of car is he looking for?" I asked Max, who was reading *Scientific American*. "Something practical? Inexpensive? Reliable?"

Max shrugged. "I don't know. Why don't you go out there and follow him around?"

"It's too hot." Even though September had come, the Florida sun was beaming down with intense energy. The parking lot was unbearable, and I could see that Dad was sweating, even though the salesman looked cool and comfortable. Bertha Blue was parked off to the side and looked lonesome.

Finally Dad and the salesman came back into the office building. "Thank you, Mr. Perkins," the salesman said, extending his hand. "If you'll just come back here to fill out the paper work, you can drive that new car home."

"What new car, Dad?" I asked. Even Max looked up in curiosity. But Dad only waved at us and followed the salesman out of the room.

I went to the window and looked out at the parking lot. There were family vans, station wagons, sedans, tiny economical cars, and one that wore a banner proclaiming it to be "environmentally unthreatening." Which one did Dad choose?

My stomach was sending out severe hunger pains by the time Dad came out of the salesman's office. He was smiling and held up two shiny keys. He dangled them in front of Max's eyes. "Anybody for lunch?" Dad asked. "Would you like to ride in style for a change?"

Max and I jumped up and followed Dad out into the parking lot. We passed the vans, the station wagons, the sedans, and the economical cars. Dad didn't even pause at the environmentally unthreatening car but walked jauntily to a red convertible with only two seats.

Max looked confused, and I was insulted. "A two-seater? Dad, where am I supposed to sit?"

"You can ride between me and Max here," Dad said, patting the hump between the seats. "And you'll love the feel of the wind in your hair. A single guy doesn't need a family car, now, does he?"

Then I realized the sick reason behind it all. Today my dad's divorce was final, so he went out and traded Bertha Blue, the old family car, for the official badge of the single guy: a sports car. Whoever said grown-ups were mature was wrong.

Max held the door open for me, so I climbed in and tried to tuck my knees under my chin. This was going to be awful. From now until forever or until this car died, either me or Max would be riding like a crane, all scrunched up.

Max, though, obviously wasn't thinking of any of this. This was his car, too. He would ride to school in it. Max climbed in beside me, slammed his door, and ran his hands over the seat. "Leather, huh, Dad?" he asked. "What'll she do on the highway?"

"She goes fast enough, Son," Dad said, turning the key and listening to the purr of the engine. He stepped on the gas a few times to let the engine roar. "Zero to sixty in 5.5 seconds."

Max beamed. "That's fast enough."

"What are we going to call her?" I asked, not sure I liked this flashy machine who had bumped poor Bertha onto a used car lot. "Lola?"

"No," Dad said, carefully backing out of the parking spot. "Something classy. Estelle."

We pulled out of the parking lot and burned rubber—Estelle, my balding father, Max, and me. Just a normal abnormal family.

3

It was a weird weekend, and I was glad to get home. Dad dropped me off at my house at six o'clock, but Mom's car wasn't in the driveway. There was a note stuck under the doormat, though, our usual hiding place. "Cass," the note said, "I'll be home by seven. I'm at the Harrises' if you need anything. Missed you!"

Dad scowled. "You mean she's not here? I'm not going to just leave you here alone!"

"It's OK, Dad," I answered, digging into my purse for my key. "I'll be fine." I knew Dad wasn't really upset about leaving me alone because I was home alone lots of times. Dad was mad because Mom had a life of her own. But what did he care? He wasn't her husband any more.

"I can't believe Claire would do this," Dad muttered under his breath, loud enough for me to hear. "I'm always home when she drops Max off."

"Max is ten, and I'm almost fourteen," I answered, opening the door. "There's a difference."

Dad was still frowning, so I stood on tiptoe and kissed his cheek. "Bye, Dad. I know where she is if I need anything. Don't worry, I'll be fine."

"Well . . ." Dad hesitated for a moment, then pushed the door open and walked past me. "Just let me walk through the house and make sure everything's OK."

Max gave Estelle's horn a beep. I peered around the corner and rolled my eyes. "Just a minute, Max," I called. "Dad's checking the house."

"For what?" Max asked, crinkling his nose.

"Who knows?" I shrugged. "Burglars or something."

I tiptoed in behind Dad and dropped my overnight bag in the living room. Dad wasn't looking for prowlers. He was walking through the living room and sneaking glances at Mom's pictures, her date book, and he even ran his finger over the stack of mail on her desk.

"Nobody's in here, Dad," I said, and he jumped.

"OK," he said, looking guilty. "But you're

sure you know where your mother is? What if you need something?"

"I know where she is, and she'll be home soon," I said, deliberately not telling him what he wanted to hear. "You don't have to worry about it."

Estelle beeped again.

"You'd better go," I reminded him. "Max is going to wear Estelle's horn out."

"OK. Take care, Gypsy Girl." Dad gave me a quick peck on the cheek, walked out, and closed the door behind him.

I leaned against the door and sighed. My father was really acting strange. Was it all because of the divorce?

Suki's getting a little up in age, and she doesn't always hear me when I come in anymore. I had just found her and given her a welcome home hug when the phone rang. "Hi, Cass?" a man's voice said. It was Tom Harris.

"Yes?"

There was a smile in his voice. "Listen, your mom's on her way home, and I forgot to tell her I got tickets for that ballet she wanted to see. Can you tell her I'll pick her up Tuesday night? I'd tell her myself, but I'm leaving to go out of town and won't be back until late Tuesday afternoon."

"OK." I remember Mom saying she wanted

to see the ballet, but two tickets would have cost more than a hundred dollars, and we couldn't afford it. Tom Harris would be spending big bucks. "Is this her birthday present?"

Tom was surprised. "When's her birthday?"

"Tomorrow."

He drew in his breath. "I'm glad you told me. Don't forget to tell her, OK? You're a sweetheart. Bye."

He hung up, and I let the phone drop out of my hand and dangle a few inches above the floor. As it spun, I thought about my father and mother and their divorce. Yes, the divorce was final now, but wasn't Dad's snooping a sign that he missed Mom? He was obviously dying to know where she was. Was he jealous? Probably. Could I get them back together? Maybe.

No one would blame me if I forgot to tell Mom about Tom Harris and the ballet. And if I could get Mom out of the house on Tuesday night at seven, then when Tom Harris showed up and no one was home, maybe he'd think she didn't want to see him anymore. He'd be too embarrassed to say anything to her, and she'd never know anything happened.

And if Dad . . . I pressed the receiver and called Dad. He wasn't home yet, so I left a message on his answering machine: "Dad, I thought I should remind you that tomorrow's

Mom's birthday. I know she'll be depressed if she doesn't hear from you and Max."

That was all I could do. Now I could only wait and see what tomorrow would bring.

After school, Miss Cason held the meeting we had all been waiting for. "The board has decided that our productions this year will be *The Crucible* by Arthur Miller; Shakespeare's *The Taming of the Shrew;* and . . ." She paused. "Our first production will be the popular musical, *The Sound of Music,*" she announced, with a flourish of her arms. "It's a marvelous play, one you're all familiar with, and with a large cast. Auditions will begin Wednesday, so if you'd like to have a performance role, you should prepare two songs and sign up promptly for an audition. The cast will be announced sometime next week."

I was so excited! *The Sound of Music* was one of my favorite movies, and when I was a kid I used to run through the backyard pretending I was Maria. I'd run through the yard singing, "The hills are alive . . ." I would give anything to be Maria!

I would have to go home and look through my music books to find two songs for the audition. I caught a city bus and hoped the driver would hurry. I had a lot to do. Not only did I have to find a song for the audition, but if Mom had been out all day, and if Dad and Tom Harris had both done what I thought they would do . . .

Nothing unusual was waiting at home. I checked the front porch, the mailbox, and Mom's office. From the looks of things, Mom had left early this morning and hadn't been home since.

I had just poured myself a Coke when the doorbell rang. I saw our next door neighbor, Mr. Bushnell, through the glass. He smiled when I opened the door.

"Today must be a special day," he said, pointing to two bouquets of flowers at his feet. "I collected these from the florist's delivery man this morning."

I couldn't have planned it better if I had ordered the flowers myself. The first bouquet was stunning, at least two dozen long-stemmed red roses in a tall crystal vase. A card was elegantly hanging from the vase, and I knew it would be from Tom Harris.

The second bouquet was small and modest; a group of daisies with a few sprigs of baby's breath. Sticking up from a plastic holder was a small typed card that read: "Happy Birthday to the best mother a child could have. Glen and Max."

I thanked Mr. Bushnell and brought the flowers inside. I carefully opened the gold foil envelope hanging from the roses. There was a typed message: "With each new day you bring new joys. Always, Tom."

Gross. Couldn't the man write anything specific? I took Dad's card out of the daisies and put it in the gold envelope. I stuck Tom's card into the plastic holder with the daisies.

There! Surely the best mother a child could have deserved roses! And someone who was writing such silly stuff as "with each new day . . ." deserved daisies.

It was at least worth a try.

Mom was pleased when she saw the flowers, and she buried her face in the roses. "How beautiful," she murmured. "And how sweet. I didn't even know he knew it was my birthday."

"Who are they from?" I asked, pretending not to know anything. "Mr. Bushnell brought them over, so I wasn't here when they were delivered."

Mom tenderly opened the foil envelope and read the enclosed card. Her eyebrows rushed together. "The best mother?" she said aloud, looking at the roses again as if they were some sort of a joke. Then she looked at the daisies, and pulled the card out of the plastic holder.

She smiled as she read it. "How sweet," she said again, this time stopping to smell the daisies, even though I knew daisies don't smell at all. She delicately fingered a sprig of baby's breath, then picked up the bouquet and carried it into her bedroom.

"Will you put the roses somewhere, Cassie?" she called. "Anywhere's fine, just as long as they don't get in the way."

Chip called that night and reminded me there was a meeting of the Main Event at his youth pastor's house if I wanted to go. Mom said it was OK, so Chip and his dad picked me up after dinner.

A few months ago, at a meeting at Doug Richlett's house, I had given my life to Christ, and I was still learning what that meant. Chip explained that Christ was living inside me now, in the form of the Holy Spirit, and that I should live my life the way Jesus wanted me to live it. As I sat in the meeting and thought about Mom's flowers, I had the feeling I had failed today. But didn't Jesus understand I was only trying to get my parents back together?

The group played a few games, and then Doug invited everyone into the living room for talking and prayer. Chip and I sat on the floor, while Doug asked if any of us had prayer requests. A couple of kids mentioned things such as sick relatives, big tests, and friends with problems.

I timidly raised my hand. "Cassie?" Doug said, nodding toward me.

"I, uh, have this uncle who has been acting

weird," I said. "He's having problems in his marriage, and he's left home. I just want to pray for my uncle—that God will fix his family so they can all be normal again."

Doug nodded. "OK, we'll pray for your uncle."

My cheeks burned. God knew I was lying; I didn't even have an uncle. But I couldn't tell the truth in front of all these kids. I just knew they came from solid, normal homes, each with a mom, a dad, kids, and a mini van.

Chip was looking at me curiously, and he raised his hand, too. "Chip?" Doug asked.

"I'd like to pray for a friend who's pretty confused," Chip said. "She's going through some rough times, and I don't want to give her name, but I'd like you all to pray for her."

"OK, we will," Doug said, nodding again. "Anyone else?"

I had forgotten that Chip knew everything about my family. He probably knew I didn't have an uncle, and he definitely knew I had been upset about my family for months. I put my head down on my knees so no one could see that I was crimson with embarrassment.

4

Mom was on the phone when I got home. "Tom, the flowers were lovely," she said, smiling at me as I came in. "It was so sweet of you to remember my birthday. So thoughtful!"

I cringed. Any minute she would say something about daisies, and Tom would say he ordered roses, and I'd be in big trouble. But she kept crooning into the phone and nothing happened.

"Tomorrow night? I'd love to go out," she said. "No, Cassie hasn't mentioned anything. Have you been planning a surprise?" She laughed. "OK, I'll be ready at seven, and you can surprise me. The whole evening's yours."

She hung up the phone and looked up at me. "Were you supposed to tell me Tom wanted to take me out tomorrow night?"

I stuttered. "It—it was a surprise. I thought

I'd wait, you know, until the last minute, so you'd be more surprised."

"Oh." Mom was still smiling. "I don't know what he's got planned, but it's sure to be something special." She took a sip of her iced tea, then snapped her fingers. "Oh, I'd better call Dad and Max, too, and thank them for the flowers."

I looked around, but didn't see the roses anywhere. "Where are they?"

"Oh, I took them over to Mrs. Conrad," Mom said, dialing Dad's number. "She loves roses so much I knew she'd enjoy them. Hello? Glen, I just wanted to thank you and Max for the flowers. They were lovely."

Her tone was clipped and polite, as if she were talking to a client. "Thank you for thinking of me. How's Max? Give him my love, OK?"

She hung up and that was it. I had lied, and cheated, and lied again . . . and all for nothing.

Mrs. Everhart taught us composition, and Tuesday's assignment was on the chalkboard: "Write about your heart's greatest desire."

"What do you mean, 'our heart's greatest desire'?" Shalisa asked. "What we want to achieve or attain?"

"Why not both?" Mrs. Everhart said. I've always hated teachers who answer a question with another question. I could never get a

34

straight answer out of Mrs. Everhart. She went on: "Is life for getting or giving? Do we strive to achieve mighty things or to attain material possessions, prominence, or excellence?"

She looked down her long nose, and her beady eyes fastened on me. "Cassiopeia, what do you think?"

"It's Cassie," I answered, "and I don't spend much time thinking about life in general."

"What do you think about?" she asked, leaning back against her desk and folding her arms.

Brother. Wasn't she going to leave me alone? "Life in specific," I answered. A couple of kids giggled in the back of the room.

"Very well," she said, standing up. "Write about life in specific, then. Your papers, which may be in any form, are due first thing tomorrow morning."

That night I realized for the first time how difficult school at the Spa could be. Someone like Max could handle it, but I couldn't. First, I had to prepare two songs for the audition, and they had to be good songs or I wouldn't stand a chance at getting to play Maria. Then I had to write the paper for Mrs. Everhart, do three pages of algebra, read a chapter of science, and study for a history test. All that, and I didn't even get home until four-thirty.

Chip called after dinner, and I told him I

couldn't talk. "I'm sorry, Chip, but I've got a load of work to do," I explained.

"Cassie, I can't believe you're taking school seriously," he teased.

I didn't blame him for doubting me. At Astronaut Junior High I was an OK student and almost always got my homework done during my study hall. "You wouldn't believe the work I have to do," I said. "Honestly. Call me tomorrow night, OK?"

I finally decided to audition with the same two songs I'd used this summer to audition for the school. I could sing those songs in my sleep, and besides, none of the songs I'd worked on in voice lessons were good enough. I didn't even know any words to put in my German song, and I didn't think the judges would be impressed by my singing "ah" the entire time.

I settled down on my bed with my pen and paper to write my English paper. I decided to make it a poem. Writing poems comes pretty easily to me because I've been keeping a secret notebook of my private thoughts since I was ten. But I have to be in a certain kind of mood to write my private poems, and now I couldn't find the mood when I needed it.

Suki came to the side of my bed and scratched her nails on the bedspread. Poor thing, she was too heavy and old to jump up anymore, so I grabbed her and heaved her over the side of the bed. She licked my cheek in appreciation, then settled down by my side to sleep while I wrote.

My heart's desire. What was my heart's desire? To get the part of Maria in the play? That would be neat, but since I had gotten the lead in my junior high musical, that wasn't my greatest heart's desire anymore.

Was it to get my mom and dad back together? I had tried that before, but when Mom and Dad were put together, they treated each other like polite strangers. They'd acted that way before they separated, and living with them wasn't fun at all.

Was my heart's desire to fall madly in love? Someday, sure. But not now. I had too many other things to worry about.

I didn't know what my heart's desire was. I didn't even know what I should want it to be. Should I want fame? Excellence? To be like Mother Teresa and give my life to helping people? Since I had given my life to Christ, shouldn't my heart's desire be something he would approve of?

Something Chip had once said came back to me now. "Cassie, when you give your life to Christ, you do your best and let him guide you," Chip had told me. "He will give you what you need."

I reached over to my nightstand and pulled out the Bible I had had for years. I flipped through the pages, reading snatches here and there, but then something caught my eye: "Delight yourself in the Lord and he will give you the desires of your heart. Commit your way to the Lord; trust in him and he will do this."

Chip must have read this verse, but I wondered if he could explain it to me a little better. How could God give me the desires of my heart when I didn't even know what I wanted?

Suddenly, I knew what I wanted, and I was ready to write my poem:

Cassie Perkins
September 4
Mrs. Everhart
Composition

My Heart's Greatest Desire

God in heaven, God above,
You gave to me your perfect love,
You said that we should love each other,
Mothers and fathers, sisters and brothers.

Since I've given my life to you,
I've promised to trust in what you do,
Although I do not understand
How this divorce is in your plan.

You've felt my hurt, you've seen my pain,
You've heard me crying in the rain,
Pull my family out of this fire—
That is my heart's greatest desire.

There. It may not have been what Mrs. Everhart was expecting, but it was honest, and that was a lot more than I had been lately. I decided that if I really wanted God to help me through this, I was going to have to stop doing things he wouldn't like. No more lying. No more plotting against Mom and Dad. No more trying to do things myself.

I couldn't make my parents get back together anyway. They were adults, and they made their own decisions. But maybe God could make the pain go away.

I was humming my song for the audition when I went into the kitchen for a glass of milk before bed. I heard the click of the front door lock, though, and froze behind a corner. Mom was home from her date with Tom Harris, and I prayed he wouldn't come in and catch me in my nightgown.

He didn't come in, thank goodness, and I heard Mom murmur something and close the door. I gulped my milk and put my glass in the sink, hoping to make it into bed before Mom saw me, but she came around the corner. "Guess what?" she said, her eyes glowing. She actually blushed and looked down at the floor. "Tonight Tom asked me to marry him."

I nearly choked. "What did you tell him?"

Mom put her hand on my cheek. "I said I'd think about it, Cassie. Now go on to bed and we'll talk about it tomorrow. Sleep tight. All our troubles are over."

I felt as though trouble were beginning all over again.

5

I couldn't sleep. Mom marry Tom Harris? Already? She's only been divorced four days, and she's already thinking about marrying someone else? Why did she think Tom Harris could take my dad's place? He couldn't, not ever.

That's what I told her the next morning when I got up. Mom was already at the kitchen counter, all wrapped up in her white terry cloth robe and drinking a cup of coffee. Her cheeks were rosy and her eyes were bright. "Good morning, honey," she said. "How did you sleep?"

I was in no mood for small talk. "I couldn't sleep at all. I just kept thinking about you marrying Tom Harris."

I was hoping she'd laugh and tell me the whole idea was crazy, that it was some sort of nightmare, but she didn't. She just put her cup of coffee down on the counter and slowly ran her fingertip around the rim. "What were you thinking?"

I took a deep breath. "I was thinking that Tom Harris could never take Dad's place. And that you've only been divorced five days. And that this is too soon and too sudden. And I don't want another dad, and I don't want to move, and I don't want Nick Harris as a brother!"

I'd said just about everything, but Mom was still smiling. "It's OK, honey, we all will need some time to get used to the idea. And no one's said we'll be moving, or what will be happening. Tom and I really haven't talked about details yet."

"When Dad left, you said it would be me and you, Mom. You said that we would do just fine with just the two of us. We could stay in the house, and I wouldn't have to move away from my friends, and we'd always have each other. Remember? You said that right after Dad left, and now you want to bring in Tom Harris? We don't need Tom Harris or his fancy house or his fancy cars."

Mom looked down and rubbed the rim of her coffee cup again. She didn't look up at me, but she said, "You've really been thinking hard about this, haven't you?"

"There was nothing else to do last night."

"Oh." She stood up, walked to the sink, and

poured what was left of her coffee into the sink. "Well, I want you to think about this. Your father and I did not have a perfect marriage, Cassie. We didn't even have a good one. We were miserable almost right from the first, but I never let you kids know anything. Your father has always loved the stars and adventure more than his family."

"You can't say that! Dad loves us! I know he does!"

Mom held up her hands in defense and closed her eyes. She took a breath and nodded. "You're right, he does love you and Max. And in a half-hearted sort of way, he loved me, too. But Cassie, a wife wants to be first in her husband's life, not second or third."

I didn't know what to say. She was telling me things I didn't want to hear, and I held my head between my hands.

"We were married on July 14, 1969," Mom went on, leaning back against the kitchen counter. "We honeymooned in Niagara Falls. On July 16, Apollo 11 was launched from Cape Kennedy, and on July 20, Neil Armstrong walked on the moon."

"So?" What was this, a history lesson?

"Your father couldn't tear himself away from the television even to spend time with me on our honeymoon. When Neil Armstrong finally walked on the moon, everyone in America cheered, including your father. He was watching on TV, and he stood up and yelled like it was a football game or something."

She looked down at the floor and her chin quivered. "When Armstrong took those first steps, I was in the bathroom crying. I knew it was a sign of things to come. Glen didn't know where I was, and worst of all, he didn't even care."

I definitely didn't want to hear any of this. Like a little kid, I put my hands over my ears.

"Your father's not a bad man," Mom said, leaning over the counter to look into my eyes, "but he's just never been able to give me what I needed. When the *Challenger* exploded, your father became totally impossible to reach. I tried everything I knew to try, and nothing worked. Our marriage was over."

"Dad still asks about you," I insisted, my tears flowing freely. I couldn't stop. "What if he wanted to come back? Wouldn't you let him?"

Mom sighed. "Cassie, he doesn't want to come back. He could have come back at any time during our separation, but he didn't. He only talks about me because he's embarrassed by the failure of the marriage."

She grabbed my hands and held them tight. Her brown eyes were inches from mine. "Honey, I don't think he'll ever change. It's not your fault, or Max's fault—it's just the way things are."

I yanked my hands from hers, mainly because I wanted to wipe the tears from my face.

"I'm sorry you had to hear this," Mom said softly, pulling away. "But I figured you have a right to know. And now that I've met a nice man, I think I have a right to find happiness. Think about that for a while, Cass."

I ran out of the room.

I deliberately put thoughts of Mom and marriage out of my mind for the rest of the week. There was school to get through, and the auditions, voice, and dance. I kept as busy as I could.

The auditions went well, I thought. At least I had as good a chance as anyone else. I sang "I Enjoy Being a Girl" and thought that Miss Cason, Mr. Levy, and Mrs. Blackwelder were impressed. But I didn't hang around to hear anyone else. Everyone at the Spa was good, and I knew I'd only get discouraged if I did.

When I finally got home on Friday afternoon, both Mom and Max were already there. Max was looking sharp in a new red and white shirt that said "I survived the Astronaut Jr. High Brain Brawl." "Hi, kiddo," I said, rumpling Max's wavy hair. "Glad to have you aboard for the weekend. How's school?"

"Fine," he said, shrugging. "You're looking at the youngest freshman at Astronaut High."

I nearly dropped my books. "You decided to go? You're in school with Andrea and Chip?"

Max nodded. "Of course, they're taking mostly freshman classes and most of mine are junior-level, but yeah, I see them in the halls a lot. They told me to tell you hi."

A wave of homesickness swept over me. Can you feel homesick for a school you've never even been in? Definitely. My friends were all there. My true friends, that is.

Mom was unwrapping something in a foil dish for dinner. "Why don't you two go outside and take a walk along the river? I'm sure you have lots to talk about."

Max and I took the hint. When we were safely out of our yard, I asked, "Did she tell you she wants to marry Tom Harris?"

"She said she was considering it," Max answered. "Does she really want to?"

"I think so." We reached the end of our street and turned the corner. On the other side of the road was the Indian River, sparkling in the sun.

Without thinking, we synchronized our footsteps and walked together on the sidewalk, avoiding the cracks. "If she marries Tom Harris, will you come to live with me and Dad?" Max asked, a glimmer of hope in his eyes.

I shrugged. "Maybe. I know Mom has custody of me, but maybe she wouldn't want me around. I know I'd rather live with you and Dad than in Tom Harris's house."

Max wasn't listening anymore; he was looking

at an old tree on the other side of the road. The tree hung out over the river. "Do you realize how deep that tree's roots must be to allow it to grow nearly sideways?" he asked, his brow wrinkled in concentration. "I want a closer look."

"Let's not," I complained. Max was always investigating something and usually got us into trouble.

He wasn't listening. He had already scampered across the street and was on the tree, about six feet over the water. "If I can estimate the radius of the trunk, I can figure its age," Max explained, leaning down to wrap his arms around the trunk. "And if I can come up with an approximate age, I can tell when the waters first encroached upon this riverbank. This tree didn't start out sideways, I'm sure."

I leaned back against a normal tree on the riverbank and tolerated Max's foolishness. He was a boy genius, and just last summer had earned twenty thousand dollars selling the recipe for Fido's Fricassee, his algae dog-food experiment. Who was I to stand in the way of science? Besides, the river was relaxing. I could see several big fish swim by in the shallow water.

"Come on, Max, hurry up," I urged, looking down as a swarm of red ants began to cover my ankle. "Ouch! I'm being eaten alive here."

I heard Max yell, then a splash. Max was no longer on the tree but under the water.

"Come on, Max, stop fooling around," I called, knowing the water was only four or five feet deep. But Max wasn't swimming. He wasn't playing. He wasn't even in sight.

I scanned the water, but all was quiet. The ripples caused by Max's splash had vanished, and the little waves continued to flow past with the river's current. I ran into the water up to my knees, a few feet downstream from Max's tree.

"Come on, Max, come up," I called again. "Stop fooling around or I'll just walk away. I'm in no mood for one of your dumb experiments."

Max didn't answer me, but from the corner of my eye I saw a red flash in the water. It was the red lettering on his T-shirt. Max was floating by. He wasn't playing.

I lunged for him, and my fingertips just caught the fabric of his shirt. With a huge yank, I pulled his head above water, but he didn't respond—no gasp, no yell, no breath. I think I was screaming, but all I remember was dragging, pulling, yanking Max out of the water and onto the riverbank.

Every muscle in Max's body was quivering. I had never seen anything like it, but it seemed like some sort of seizure. His legs, his arms, even his facial muscles twitched and jerked. I couldn't tell if he was breathing.

I knelt on the ground, dripping wet, and hugged my knees and screamed. Wouldn't anybody come?

A man from the house across the street rushed over. "I saw the whole thing from my yard," he said. "I called 911. It's OK, help is on the way."

He looked at Max and was as confused as I was. I knew that if someone was drowning you were supposed to give artificial respiration, but I'd never heard of anyone twitching like this. What on earth was happening to my brother?

"Do you live near here?" the man was asking me.

I nodded.

"Go home and tell your mother what has happened. She will need to go to the hospital before they can do anything. I'll watch him until the paramedics get here. Now run!"

I ran like the wind, snatching breaths as my sobs echoed in my ears and my feet pounded the pavement. Max was dying, and all I could do was run.

6

By the time Mom and I got to the hospital's emergency room, Max was sitting up on one of those stretcher beds, wet, but smiling. He wasn't dead. In fact, he was looking around intently and asking the doctor about all the instruments and what they did.

Mom turned pale with relief, and I thought she'd faint. All I'd been able to say was "Mom—Max—drown—twitching—ambulance—hospital," and she'd pulled me out the door and into the car. Now here we were, and everything was OK.

Or was it? Why did Max fall off that tree? "He must have slipped and hit his head on something in the water," Mom said, smiling in relief. "And you got him out in time, Cassie. You saved his life."

I walked over to a chair against the wall and

practically fell into it. I let my head thump against the back wall. When Max was better, I was going to kill him. Or if he ever scared me like that again, *then* I'd kill him. Having a brother was going to give me fits.

The doctor came over to me. "You were with your brother?"

I nodded.

"Did you see him fall?"

"No." I looked down at my tennis shoes. "I had looked away for a minute. Red ants were biting me."

"Did you hear him shout? Did he say anything about seeing colors or smelling anything?"

I crinkled my forehead, trying to remember. "I think he yelled, then I heard a splash. That was all."

The doctor smiled at Mom. "Mrs. Perkins, I'd like to keep Max here for some tests," he said. "Ordinarily, I'd assume he was knocked unconscious momentarily by something in the water, but there are no marks, bruises, or bumps on his head. And I understand he only fell a distance of about four feet."

I nodded. "That's right."

"What are you thinking, doctor?" Mom was frowning.

"I want to be sure, but from what I've heard, and my preliminary examination, I think we're looking at epilepsy."

"Epilepsy?" Mom abruptly sank into the chair next to me.

"Yes. Why don't you go along to the admissions office so we can run some tests. We'll have some answers for you by Monday."

On Monday afternoon after she and Dad met with the doctor, Mom told me that epilepsy is a symptom, not a disease. The seizures come when electrically unstable brain cells sort of overload in the brain. Seizures like Max's only last from two to five minutes and can usually be prevented with medication.

"Why does he have epilepsy?" I asked. "Does it run in our family, or did he get it from one of his experiments?"

"Neither," Mom said. "It could be because of a high fever he had when he was a baby, or a chemical imbalance, or a brain tumor. But the doctors did a CAT scan of his brain, and they're fairly sure there is no tumor. They think Max is just going to have to live with this."

I shuddered. For the last two nights I had been having nightmares about Max lying in the grass, smeared with mud, and jerking uncontrollably. In my dreams I ran, ran, ran, trying to get away. Mom was lucky she wasn't there when it happened.

"Anyway," Mom went on, "since the doctors have ruled out a brain tumor, they say it's likely he'll outgrow the seizures by the time he hits puberty. The most important thing is that we treat him as normally as we can. Stress and instability aren't good for him."

She bit her lip nervously, and I wondered if she thought her news about remarrying had stressed Max out. Maybe it had. Marrying Tom Harris certainly wouldn't bring any stability into Max's life—not as far as I could see.

Mom turned away from me. "I need to call Tom," she said, mostly to herself. "Just to hear his voice."

That night I called Max. "Hi, Whiz Kid," I teased him. "How does it feel to be home?"

"Great," Max answered. "Hospitals are interesting for a while, but after that, it's boring. They wouldn't even let Dad bring in my laptop computer."

"Poor thing." I laughed. "So, what's up?"

"I've been doing research," Max went on, "and I'm convinced that epilepsy is not only an electrical overload of the brain cells, or a surge, so to speak, but that such instances, if properly controlled, could be beneficial."

"What?" As usual, I was lost in his explanation.

"What if electrically sensitive brains, such as those of epileptics, are more responsive to stimuli?" he asked.

"Come again?"

"What if epileptics are more intelligent?" Max

bellowed. "Did you know that Alexander the Great, Julius Caesar, Handel, Dante, Tchaikovsky, Van Gogh, Dostoevsky, and Alfred Nobel all had epilepsy?"

"They did?" I didn't know who half of those guys were, but I knew they had to be important or Max wouldn't have mentioned them.

"Yes. And now you can add the name of Maxwell Brian Perkins to the list."

I had been worried that Max would feel embarrassed or upset by what the doctor said, but he was using it as a claim to fame. Max would be fine.

"I think that's wonderful," I assured him. "Just be sure to take your medicine, OK? I won't always be there to pull you out of trouble if you—" I paused, not wanting to say the word.

"Have another seizure. It's OK, Cassie. I've probably been having seizures for years."

"No way."

"Yeah. There's another kind of seizure, called a petit mal seizure, where epileptics just stare off into space for a few seconds."

"You know, you've been doing that all your life." I giggled. "I just thought it was your boy genius expression."

Max sighed. "I know. We geniuses are so misunderstood."

"Give me a break. Well, I'll see you at Dad's this weekend, OK? So long, Genius."

7

It seemed kind of rotten, but all of a sudden I realized that Max's epilepsy might be just the thing to keep Tom Harris from marrying my mother. What if he was a big chicken and didn't want the responsibility? What had Mom told Tom about it? Had she told him anything at all?

I decided not to wait until Mom had a chance to break the news to him gently. On Monday night at about eleven-thirty, after Mom had gone to bed, I reached for my telephone and dialed the Harrises' number. It didn't matter who answered the phone. I could drop this bomb on anyone: Nick, Uncle Jacob, or even Tom himself.

Uncle Jacob answered the phone in his usual gruff voice. "Harris residence," he growled, "and this had better be an emergency."

I gathered my courage to put on the acting

performance of my life. "Uncle Jacob?" I squeaked, trying to sound frightened. "I just have to talk to someone. It's horrible news, and Mom's gone to bed because she can't handle it."

"Cassie?" Uncle Jacob recognized my voice. His voice softened. "What's wrong, Missy?"

I almost hesitated because I really liked Uncle Jacob and hated to do this to him. But he was one of "them," and if I didn't do this and do it well, I'd be one of them, too, in a few months. I'd rather die than be part of the Harris household.

"It's Max," I blubbered. "He's got epilepsy, and the really bad kind, too. He fell in the river Friday night and was in the hospital all weekend. I saw him, Uncle Jacob! He twitched and jerked and nearly drowned, and we've got to live with this for the rest of our lives. It's terrible!"

Uncle Jacob clicked his tongue in sympathy and murmured, "Poor Max."

"Poor Mom!" I moaned. "She's so upset, she's falling to pieces. She's afraid Tom won't want Max around since he's going to be sick forever, and she can't bear to never see Max again."

Since I had stretched the truth and seemed to be getting away with it, I let go of it altogether. "My parents are talking about institutionalizing Max, and you know how expensive that is! Dad can't afford to pay for it, and if Mom marries Tom, why, Tom will have to pay thousands and thousands of dollars for poor Max. It's just terrible, Uncle Jacob."

Uncle Jacob was silent, and I imagined him sitting there with his hand on the phone, wondering how on earth he could convince Tom Harris not to marry Claire Perkins. Finally he spoke: "Missy . . . " He paused. "You're really having a hard time realizing that your mom's in love with Tom, aren't you?"

I was shocked. He didn't believe me. What had I done wrong?

"What?" I pretended not to understand. "Max has epilepsy. I'm not making this up, Uncle Jacob. He fell in the river, and I saved his life, but he scared me and Mom to death."

"I know," Uncle Jacob said simply. "Your mother already called Tom and told us the news. She also said that Max would be fine, and his seizures could be controlled with medication. She sounded as calm and cool as a cucumber. Tom wanted to go to the hospital himself, but your mother said Max was absolutely fine."

"Oh." I felt like a little kid who'd been caught with her hand in the cookie jar.

Uncle Jacob spoke again. "It's OK, Missy. I think I understand why you're afraid. But things will be OK. Trust me."

I was embarrassed. Uncle Jacob was a nice guy, and I'd lied to him and made a fool of myself. "I'm sorry," I blubbered, this time for real. "Please don't . . ."

"I won't say anything about this," he promised. "Now go on to sleep. Good night." The phone clicked, and I lay back against my pillow while hot tears ran down my face. How humiliated could I be? It was all Tom Harris's fault. Boy, was he ever a jerk.

Miss Cason kept her promise and posted the cast announcements for *The Sound of Music* on the bulletin board outside her office. Everyone else in school was buzzing around the announcement, but I was too depressed to even look. I probably had been assigned to paint backdrops.

But Shalisa ran over and grabbed my arm. "Congratulations, Cassie, you got a really plum role," she squealed, practically hugging me. "Just think, we'll be singing solos together in the first production of the year! It will be an honor to sing with you!"

"Yeah, yeah," I muttered under my breath as she rushed on to congratulate the next superstar who was privileged enough to sing with her. But I was curious. A solo part? Did I get the part of Maria?

I stood on tiptoe, wishing I were five inches taller. At the top of the page I read:

Maria von Trapp: Shalisa McRay

So Shalisa was the star. Fine. Maybe I got the part of one of the children—they sang fun songs and were in all the biggest scenes. But no, my name wasn't anywhere. I wasn't Louisa, Liesl, Brigitta, Marta, or Gretl. I finally spotted my name near the end of the list.

The Reverend Mother: Cassiopeia Perkins

The Reverend Mother! I was going to play an old, wrinkled nun who walked around in a hot costume with her hands folded in her sleeves all day. The only good thing about the Reverend Mother's part was the solo, "Climb Ev'ry Mountain." But in character I probably wouldn't smile, I wouldn't laugh, and I certainly wouldn't dance. This was going to be loads of fun.

There was one other good thing about the part. The costume was black, and at the moment, black certainly fit my mood.

I was glad when Dad pulled up with Max in red-hot Estelle, even though I had to sit between them with the gear shift digging into my leg. I'd have run along behind them to get away from Mom. All week she'd been smiling and looking through a new copy of *Modern Bride.* It was disgusting! Women her age shouldn't be planning weddings and looking at white dresses! I didn't know if she would actually wear one, but she had been gawking at the pictures a lot.

I wasn't planning on saying anything to Dad, but apparently Max had let it slip. We were in the booth at Dad's favorite Italian restaurant when he put down his menu and asked me, "So what's this I hear about your mother? Is she really getting married?"

He said it with sort of a laugh, as if he were making a joke, but his eyes were serious and a little worried. I put down my menu, too, and shrugged. "I hope not, but it looks like it. The other day I heard her ask a florist if orchids were available in December."

"That call could have been for a client," analytical Max pointed out.

"I don't think so," I snapped. "Because then she asked for the price for orchids in bouquets. It sounds like a wedding to me."

Dad ran his hand over his face and scratched his chin thoughtfully. "You know, sometimes I miss her," he said, finally.

This was it! "There's still time, Dad," I yelped, practically jumping up in my seat. "She hasn't promised Tom anything yet. Call her! Take her out to dinner! Send her flowers again!"

Max raised an eyebrow and looked from me to Dad, then back at me again. "Cassie," he whispered, a warning in his voice, "is this smart?"

I kicked Max under the table and looked Dad straight in the eye. "I think she's free Sunday night, Dad," I encouraged him. "You could call and say you want to talk about Max—"

"Leave me out of this," Max interrupted.

"And have her meet you at that little Chinese place she likes. When you get there, tell her you miss her and that you want to—well, whatever you want to do." I didn't want to rush Dad, but I didn't want him to lose Mom forever, either.

Dad picked up his menu again because the waitress was heading our way. "Maybe I will," he said, winking at me.

Dad dropped me back at Mom's house early Sunday morning because he had to work, he said. I reminded him not to be late meeting Mom for dinner. We'd both been surprised that she had agreed to come. But then again, she thought it was a meeting to talk about Max.

It was only nine o'clock, and I remembered that Chip had asked me to go to church with him lots of times, but I was usually either with Max or at Dad's. I called him up and asked if the invitation still stood. "Sure, Cassie," he said. "We'll pick you up in ten minutes."

I had just enough time to unpack my overnight bag and slip into a comfortable shirt and skirt. Mr. and Mrs. McKinnon were smiling, as usual, when I climbed into the car. "So good to see you, Cassie, dee-ah," Mrs. McKinnon said in her heavy Southern accent. "How do you like your new schoo-all?"

"It's nice," I answered. "I just got the part of the Reverend Mother in *The Sound of Music*."

"Hey, that's great," Chip said, taking my hand. "You'll be my little singing nun."

I rolled my eyes, but when Chip was holding my hand, honestly, I could feel great about anything. Even playing the part of an old nun seemed too wonderful for words.

The glow lasted all through church. Chip's Sunday school class wasn't at all like those little groups I remembered when my family used to go to church years ago. In a large room, Chip's youth pastor, Doug Richlett, led us in music, games, and skits. And then he talked to us. I looked around. There were probably a hundred kids in the room, but most were listening to Doug a lot better than they listened in school. I sat up and listened hard.

"I want to read you a verse in the Bible, Jeremiah 29:11," Doug said. He picked up his worn-out Bible and read: "'For I know the plans I have for you,' says the Lord. 'They are plans for good and not for evil, to give you a future and a hope.'"

Doug closed his Bible and looked around the room. "A lot of you are worried about tomorrow," he said, "and you'll spend all your time and energy trying to make things right when what you really need to do is trust the Lord. There's an old saying that most people spend their time wishing for things they could have if they didn't spend all their time wishing."

Doug turned and looked right at me. "Jesus came into this world so that you could be adopted by the heavenly Father," he explained. I knew that. Just a few months ago, I gave my life to God and knew that my life belonged to him. "If you are a child of God, you can trust your heavenly Father. Put all of your life into his hands, not just part of it. Because he has good plans for you, plans to give you hope and a future."

Doug sat on a stool in the front of the room and leaned toward us, his elbows on his knees. "Don't let yourself get caught up in wasting your time worrying about things that wouldn't be a problem if you didn't worry about them," he said. "God wants you to trust him. He has your best interests at heart because he really loves you."

Doug lowered his head and began talking to God, then, and I lowered my head, too, mainly because I was embarrassed. I knew Doug hadn't known I was even coming, but I felt as though he were talking right to me. I'd done some pretty rotten things in the last few weeks, things that weren't like me at all. I'd lied and tricked my mom, and manipulated people and . . .

"Forgive me, God," I whispered. "I'm sorry. If you really want this mess, you can have it."

8

That night Mom got dressed and left for the Chinese restaurant. "I'll be back in an hour," she said as she left. "Your father wants to talk about Max in private, I guess. If Tom calls, take a message, please?"

I nodded. I really would take a message, too, no matter how tempted I was to "forget" that he'd called.

But Mom was back in only half an hour. She came in and quietly shut the door behind her. I peeked around the corner. "Back so soon?"

"Your father stood me up," she said quietly, putting her purse into her favorite wing chair. "There was a table reserved, so I sat there, expecting him any minute, of course. Every five minutes or so the waiter would come and ask if I wanted to order, and I felt dumb sitting there doing nothing, so I ordered an iced tea and kept having it refilled."

She smiled and shook her head. "After five or six glasses, I couldn't hold another drop, so I paid my check and came home. I don't know what your father wants to say that he can't say over the phone, anyway."

There was a knock at the door, and I had a sinking feeling I knew who it was. Mom knew, too, because she sighed and straightened her shoulders as she opened the door.

It was Dad. "Claire, I'm sorry," he said, waving his hands helplessly. "I was working on a project at work and got so caught up I let the time slip by."

"It's OK, Glen," Mom said, smiling a tight little smile. "What did you want to talk about? Something about Max?"

"No, not exactly."

"Cassie?"

"No." Dad looked down at his feet. "I wanted to talk about us."

"There is no us, Glen," Mom said firmly, taking a step backward. "I don't know if there ever was."

I ducked back around the corner into the living room, feeling like an eavesdropper. Another brilliant idea had backfired on me.

Mom grabbed the handle of the door. "I'd be happy to discuss the children with you if there's ever a problem," she said crisply, "but we can talk on the telephone. If there's anything else, you can talk to my lawyer. Good-bye."

I lay back on the couch, feeling guilty because I'd put Dad up to this, and now he was standing out on the doorstep feeling stupid. But how could he forget to show up? How could he have let his work be more important than Mom again? Just this morning I had reminded him twenty times not to be late.

It was all Tom Harris's fault. If Mom hadn't been so hung up on him, she'd have waited an extra ten minutes for Dad, and they would have talked. He would have told her he missed her, and they would have worked things out. Once again, it was all Tom Harris's fault.

But I had promised God that I was going to stay out of it. God was just going to have to show Mom that Tom Harris was responsible for this entire mess.

Mom was bright-eyed at breakfast the next morning. "Tom stopped by last night after you went to bed," she said, pouring her usual bowl of Special K. "I agreed to marry him, and we've set the date. December 24, Christmas Eve. Won't that be lovely?"

I looked up in shock, but she didn't even notice. "We'll have to get busy and plan the wedding, honey," she said, her words flowing out on a wave of excitement. "It'll be fun! We want it tasteful, of course, but Tom wants it to be really nice. We'll have it at his house and trim everything in evergreens. You and I can come down that big spiral staircase. Won't it be gorgeous?"

She crinkled her nose in delight, and I stirred my Lucky Charms. Oh, brother. Was this the wonderful plan God had for me? My mother was going to marry The Jerk?

"And Cassie—" Mom reached out and held my hand. "Tom and I want you to sing at the wedding. Something romantic, like 'The Wind beneath My Wings.'"

I made a face, not because of the song, but at the idea of singing at Tom Harris's wedding. Mom misunderstood. "You don't like that song? All right, then, you choose something nice. Just make sure it's not, you know, too rocky." She gave my hand a squeeze. "Remember that we're older people, OK?"

She let go of my hand and was about to take a mouthful of cereal, but I had to know something. "Mom?"

"Yes, honey?" Her spoon hung in midair.

"Why are you marrying Tom Harris?"

Mom put her spoon down with a clunk and frowned for a split second. Then she looked down at her left hand. For the first time I saw the ring with its huge diamond. Mom smiled at the ring, and slowly turned it with the fingers of her right hand.

"Why am I marrying Tom Harris? Because he is thoughtful and considerate," she said softly, "and he cares about what I think. He has an outstanding reputation in the community, and he's a good provider for his family. He'll be a good father figure for you and Max, and a wonderful friend for me."

She looked up again, and her brown eyes twinkled. "Plus, Uncle Jacob will do the cooking so I won't have to. Does that answer your question?"

I looked down at the marshmallow shapes bobbing in my bowl: yellow moons, green clovers, and pink hearts. "I thought you weren't supposed to get married unless you were in love."

Mom reached out and ran her hand over my hair. "Silly girl, what do you think love is?" The phone rang, and she jumped up to answer it. "That'll be Tom. We're meeting Uncle Jacob for lunch to plan the reception and choose a caterer."

Tom was "thoughtful and considerate," and just yesterday Dad acted thoughtless and rude. Why did Tom Harris have to look so good to Mom? He only made Dad look bad in comparison.

Halfway through geometry class on Wednesday, I decided I wanted to go back to Astronaut High School. The School for the Performing Arts was not the place for me. The work was hard, the teachers were disinterested, and the other kids weren't friendly. They weren't really snobby, it was just that everyone else seemed to be in his or her own world, and no one talked to anyone else. It was a school of introverts.

Except for Shalisa. Shalisa was outgoing, charming, and my best friend at the Spa—but Shalisa was about as deep as a coat of nail polish. I wouldn't ever tell her my problems because I knew she wouldn't understand. I think her biggest problem in life is figuring out what to wear each morning, but then again, she probably has a maid to lay everything out for her.

So, I figured I'd stick this year out and be in

the three productions of this school year, even if I only worked on costumes. *The Crucible* and *The Taming of the Shrew* are dramas, not musicals, and I probably wouldn't get a part because my acting isn't nearly as good as my singing. I'm on scholarship anyway, so I might as well enjoy the voice lessons and everything. But next year, I decided I'd ask Mom if I could transfer to Astronaut High where my friends and Max are. It would be wonderful to be in class with Andrea and Chip again.

I hardly ever get to see either of them anymore. Andrea and I were practically Siamese twins until this year, and Chip and I—well, I guess we're boyfriend and girlfriend, but I'm not real sure about that. He calls when he can, but for all I know he has a girlfriend at school, too. I don't think he'd go out on me, but some girl could be chasing him, and I'd never know about it.

So I want to go to Astronaut High. For sure. But Mom will probably be married by next year, and what if Tom Harris wants me to stay at the Spa? He is the school's lawyer and on the board of directors. If Mom actually marries him, could he control my life?

"Cassie Perkins?" Mr. Granger's voice interrupted my thoughts.

"What?" Someone behind me snickered; it was obvious I wasn't paying attention.

"Can you come up to the board and work this problem? Or would you like to do several extra exercises for homework tonight?"

"I can't work the problem," I answered, thinking it was too bad Max wasn't around to do the problems for me. "But I wouldn't like extra homework tonight. I have play practice until five and at least three hours of other work to do."

Mr. Granger's nose literally went up in the air. "Students at this school are expected to do above average work," he said. "You must find the time to do what is required."

"Oh yeah?" Something in me snapped. "Well, most students at this school don't have to help their mothers run a business just to put food on the table. And the other kids at this school don't have to drive forty-five minutes to get here, because they all live in this snotty neighborhood. And the other students at this school come from fancy academies where they never had anything to do but study, so they're ready for this stuff, but I'm not! I have friends! I have a life!"

I was quivering all over, and Mr. Granger was red in the face, but I didn't care. Out of the corner of my eye I could see Shalisa's face, and her mouth was open so wide I could see the rubber bands on her invisible braces.

"Miss Perkins, you are dismissed to the dean's

office," Mr. Granger snapped, bobbing his head up and down.

"Thank you very much," I snapped back. I gathered my books and left.

I had to sit outside the dean's office on a leather sofa for nearly twenty minutes. I think they do that on purpose, because during the twenty minutes, my anger melted away and I began to feel bad. I had never in my life yelled at a teacher before. My mom would have fainted if she had seen me. Even Max would have been shocked. Andrea would have stood up and cheered. And Chip? Chip probably would be a little disappointed in me.

Melissa McMiller, a teacher's aide, saw me sitting there and made a point of bumping me, dropping papers on my head, or giving me dirty looks every time she passed by in the hall. She was a senior and totally beloved by all the teachers. She was also a total narc who really had it in for me.

The only time I had ever seen any kind of spontaneous fun at the Spa was in our biology class. The teacher had stepped out for a minute, and our resident violin prodigy, Edward Tolbert, picked up his dissection frog and began waltzing with it around the room.

Well, everybody picked up their frogs (I did, too, but I only held him by his fingertips) and began dancing them around when the prowling

76

Melissa McMiller stuck her head in the room and snapped, "That will be five demerits for each of you. I'm reporting you to the dean as required by the honor code." I walked over to Melissa and held my frog up in her face. She didn't even flinch. I was tempted to throw it on her, but knew I'd get in trouble, so I settled for something childish, but effective. I stuck my tongue out at her and walked away.

And now Melissa McMiller was holding the dean's door open and saying, "Cassie Perkins, Dean Elliot will see you now." I stood up, threw my shoulders back, and marched through the door. But not before stepping squarely on Melissa McMiller's dainty toes.

"Cassie, I don't know what's gotten into you," Mom said after reading Dean Elliot's letter. "Insubordination? Lack of attention? No discipline? This just doesn't sound like you, Cass."

"I'm sorry, Mom," I muttered. "I just don't feel like I belong there at the Spa."

Mom leaned back in her chair, exasperated. "After all we went through to get you into that school? It was all you talked about this summer! The audition, the scholarship, the performances . . ."

"I still want to be in the performances, or I'd quit now," I said quietly. "But I don't think I fit in there, Mom."

Mom sat up straighter, and her voice became firmer. "You will not quit," she said, folding the letter and sliding it back into the envelope. "When you begin something, I expect you to finish it. You will finish out the year."

"But next year, can I go back to Astronaut?"

Mom shook her head. "I don't know. I'll have to talk to your father—" She caught herself. "And Tom. We'll talk about that later. But do you think you can get through the first grading period without destroying the place?"

She stood up and walked off, angry and frustrated, and I didn't feel much better.

10

"Why don't you call your friends and go to the beach this weekend?" I knew Mom was trying to be helpful and probably trying to take some of the pressure off of me. "You can call Andrea and Chip, and Max will be here, of course. I'll drop you off at your favorite spot." She pulled out her picnic basket from under the kitchen sink. "You should call Nick, too."

I sighed. "Mom, I don't like Nick anymore. Andrea doesn't like him, either. She's found a new boyfriend at school, Brian somebody-or-other."

Mom shook her head. "I'm not trying to fix you up with Nick as a boyfriend, honey. I want you to get to know him as a brother."

She was serious. I had thought about it, sure. Mom would marry Tom Harris, and Nick would be there, too—but as my brother? No way. Nick Harris would never be my brother like Max.

"Do I have to invite Nick?"

Mom was firm. "Yes, you do. That's the whole idea."

I groaned. So she didn't suggest this outing out of her motherly concern for me; she did it for Nick Harris. How low! At least she would let me invite Andrea and Chip, too. If Nick got to be too repulsive, I could always walk away with my friends.

It was a little awkward at first. Mom and Tom deposited all of us on the beach with our towels, blankets, cooler, and picnic basket with a promise to pick us up in three hours. Max nodded solemnly, glancing up at the sky, and remarked, "Good. A storm front is approaching from the southwest. It should be here in four hours."

Nick laughed and rumpled Max's hair. "Is he for real?" he asked.

"Yes," I snapped defensively. "And if Max says it's going to rain in four hours, it will rain in four hours." Max smiled at me and took off for the water.

"Hey, I didn't mean anything," Nick said, watching Max go. "I just think he's cute."

"Cute?" I couldn't believe what I was hearing. Didn't Nick understand Max at all? "Was Einstein cute? Is Max's invention for Fido's Fricassee merely cute? It earned him twenty thousand dollars, you know."

"I know," Nick said, holding his hands up.

"Let's call a truce, OK? I want to have a good time." He leaned toward me and whispered: "Just one thing: did he take his medicine? I'd die if he had an attack—"

"Max is fine," I snapped, turning away. "You don't have to worry about him."

Nick turned to help Andrea spread out her beach blanket and I saw that Chip had been watching and listening. "I'm sorry that Nick had to come along," I said quietly so that only Chip would hear. "It was my mother's idea."

"I understand," Chip said, taking my blanket from me and shaking it out over the sand. "But Cassie, don't you think you're giving Nick a hard time?"

"A hard time?" I had thought that maybe Chip would be jealous of Nick, but here he was sticking up for the guy.

"Yeah, I mean, he's going to be your stepbrother. You'd be better off if you learned to get along."

Was the whole world going to lecture me? I stalked off to get the cooler, and I heard Nick ask Chip to toss a Frisbee with him. Great. Everyone loved Nick. Everyone but me.

An hour later I was still upset. I lay on my blanket, pretending to sleep, while Andrea and Nick talked quietly on her blanket and Chip and Max dug around in the sand by the water for sand crabs. Everything was so unfair. Chip and Andrea were *my* friends, but Nick had walked right in and made himself at home. He was having a better time with my friends than I was!

I scowled and raised myself up on my elbows to look out at the beach. Nick and Andrea were laughing and talking only a few feet away, but the wind was blowing off the water and I couldn't hear what they were saying. They were probably laughing at me or saying I was having a pity party.

"Hey, Andrea, what happened to Brian what's-his-name?" I called over my shoulder. It'd serve her right if she was embarrassed. Flirting with the enemy was almost unforgivable.

"Who are you talking about?" she yelled back. She looked over at Nick, smiled, and tossed her blonde hair.

It was disgusting. I looked away from them and watched people on the beach. A group of girls walked by, and I couldn't help but notice that they gave more than a quick glance at both Nick and Chip. They were older girls, too, probably high school or even college, and one of them even put her fingers in her mouth and whistled at Chip. He ignored her, but I felt sort of pleased and jealous at the same time. He was good-looking, tall, and golden-haired, with eyes more blue than the Atlantic.

But when another girl playfully kicked sand

on Nick, I was puzzled. Yeah, I guess he was cute. In fact, I once had had a crush on him myself. But couldn't they see how obnoxious he was? He was so spoiled!

Andrea glared at the girls, so they giggled and walked on down the beach. Andrea decided she'd had enough. "Come on, Cassie, let's go in the water," she said, glancing over toward me. "You, too, Nick. You can wash that sand off."

"I want to get some sun," I answered, lying down on my back. "You two go."

I closed my eyes and heard them walk off, but a few minutes later I could feel someone's shadow blocking the sun across my eyelids. "Please move," I said, exasperated.

"OK," a voice answered. It was Nick.

I opened my eyes and raised up on my elbows again. "I thought you wanted to swim."

"I did, but I thought we should talk. Cassie, I always thought you were a real sensible girl."

"I am."

"Well—" He shook his head and smiled. "You're not acting like it."

I gritted my teeth and was about to yell, but Nick put his hand up. "Just hear me out, OK? My dad wants to marry your mom. That's fine with me. I like your mom, and Dad's been a widower for ten years. Even Uncle Jacob likes your mom, so I'm happy they're getting married."

"Good for you."

"Aren't you?"

I didn't know what to say. Was I happy? No. Could I stop it? No. Plus, I had promised God that I wouldn't try.

"I'm still trying to get used to the idea."

"Oh." Nick sat down on the empty spot of my blanket. "We'll be brother and sister, you know."

"*Step*brother and *step*sister."

He saluted me. "Thanks for pointing that out."

"I don't have to like it, you know."

Nick ignored me and looked out across the ocean. "You can do whatever you want to."

"Well, look at the changes we're going to have to make. I'll have to move, and I've lived close to Andrea all my life. I want to go back to Astronaut next year, and I don't want to go to that academy you go to or to the Spa. Max will come to visit every other weekend, and I *like* to mess around in the kitchen. Uncle Jacob probably won't let me."

How could I explain what I meant? Giving up our house, with our pictures and our TV, and those dumb ceramic gifts that we made Mom when we were in elementary school—how could we take the flavor of our house when we moved?

"We'll have to make changes too, you know," Nick said.

"Like what?"

84

Nick shrugged. "Well, we're clearing out one of the guest rooms for you. And Dad will have to empty a closet or two to make room for all your mom's stuff."

"Some sacrifice."

He went on: "The other day Uncle Jacob was griping that he'd have to buy female stuff for you two when he goes to the store. He said it would be pretty embarrassing for a guy his age."

I was embarrassed, too, and infuriated. "Female stuff? How stupid you men are! You can just tell Uncle Jacob that I'll buy my own stuff, thank you. And if all you're doing is clearing out a guest room and emptying a closet, then you've got no idea what's really going on here, Nick Harris."

I stood up and jerked the edge of my blanket. It wouldn't budge because Nick was still sitting on it, but it did raise a cloud of sand, most of which went flying onto Nick.

"I wouldn't live with you if you paid me," I yelled, not caring who heard. "I'll just call my dad and move in with him and Max. Better to visit you on weekends than have you worry about having female stuff around all week!"

That night Max, Suki, and I sat in the living room watching TV and eating popcorn. I was sunburned and tired, and still mad at Nick, Andrea, and even Chip. After I'd yelled at Nick,

Andrea had tried to get me to apologize, which I hadn't, and Chip had tried to apologize for me by telling Nick I was under a lot of pressure. What did he know?

When Mom and Tom picked us up, everyone was smiling except me, so Tom probably thought I was having "female problems" or that it was that time of the month. Honestly! How could Mom and I move in with a houseful of men we didn't even know? The idea was repulsive and a little scary.

I hadn't been paying any attention to the movie, but Max had, so I waited until a commercial to ask, "So, do you think Dad will let me move in with you two?"

Max was surprised. "You really want to?"

"Yeah, I've been thinking about it. Why not?"

Max raised an eyebrow and shrugged, thinking. "There are advantages and disadvantages," he said, finally. "But the most important consideration is your school. Dad wouldn't be able to take you all the way over to the School for the Performing Arts, so you'd have to ride the bus to Astronaut with me."

"That's fine with me. I want to switch schools anyway."

"I thought you wanted to be a performer."

"I do." I sighed. A few months ago, I'd wanted more than anything to be a professional singer, to be in plays, on Broadway, to become a star.

I loved music and wanted to really work hard on it. But now I only wanted to get out of this marriage mess.

I reached for a handful of popcorn and tossed Suki a big, fluffy kernel. "I'm the Reverend Mother in *The Sound of Music*," I told Max. "It's not a very big part."

"It's not exactly a little part, either," Max pointed out. "It's a medium-sized part."

I shrugged. "Mom also wants me to sing at the wedding," I said, mumbling through a mouthful of popcorn. "I think I'll sing 'The Way We Were' and dedicate it to Dad."

"You wouldn't," Max said, laughing. "Mom would kill you."

"I know." I tossed another piece of popcorn to Suki. "So do you think Dad would let me move in with you two?"

Max shook his head. "You can't, Cassie, and you really don't want to. You'd be sorry if you gave up your Reverend Mother part, and besides, Dad's condominium doesn't allow dogs."

I looked down at Suki, who sat there smiling and waiting for another bite of popcorn. Max was right. I really did want to perform, badly enough to stick out my year at the Spa. And I couldn't give up Suki. No way.

I tossed her another piece of popcorn. "Oh, well. It was just an idea."

11

Melissa McMiller delivered a note to my first-period class on Monday morning, and the teacher handed it to me. "Cassiopeia Perkins," I read, "you are hereby placed on academic and disciplinary probation. Any further disturbances reported by any teacher or faculty member will result in your dismissal from the current school production." Dean Elliot's signature was scrawled across the bottom of the page.

Brother, I thought, sticking the note into my English book. *If they kicked me out of school, I wouldn't mind. But I don't want to lose my part in the play.*

I knew I'd have to be careful not to blow up at anyone else. Playing the part of the Reverend Mother wasn't the greatest dramatic challenge, but the song was worth it. Mrs. Blackwelder and I had begun to work on it in my voice lessons, and there was something majestic about "Climb Ev'ry Mountain." Mrs. Blackwelder said it was a compliment to be trusted with that song. It wasn't an easy song to sing.

So in geometry I didn't even glance at Mr. Granger but kept my eyes either on the chalkboard or in my book and dutifully scratched away in my math notebook. I was a model student.

Shalisa came toward me at lunchtime. "Can I sit here?" she asked, motioning toward the empty seat.

I shrugged. "Sure."

She sat down and daintily opened her bottle of sparkling citrus water. "I had lunch with the Harrises on Saturday at our club," she said, glancing up at me, "and I heard something that really upset me."

"What was that, Shalisa?" I didn't really want to hear about the Harrises and the McRays at their country club.

"Well . . ." Shalisa paused and blushed almost on cue. "Someone said that perhaps you were hurt because you didn't get the part of Maria in the production. Someone seemed to think that perhaps it is jealousy that's causing you to be so, well, moody lately."

She smiled and reached for my hand. "Cassie, I want you to know you have a beautiful voice

and a lot of talent. I really believe in you. Someday you'll get a starring role, I'm sure of it."

First I wanted to clobber Nick Harris because
he had to be the "someone" who blabbed to
Shalisa. Then I wanted to pick up my lunch
tray and dump it in Shalisa's lap, but Melissa
McMiller would be sure to report me to Dean
Elliot. So, instead, I smiled and pulled my hand
away from hers. "Thanks, Shalisa. That makes
me feel a lot better."

"I hope so." Shalisa beamed and unfolded a
napkin to place in her lap. "We are getting to be
such good friends, aren't we? We can be really
honest with each other."

I nodded, but left the rest of my lunch in my
lunch bag. I'd throw everything else away. I
had completely lost my appetite.

That night I didn't get home until six-thirty.
Play practice was hard. Miss Cason was very
strict about her nuns' behavior, and she made
us practice walking for nearly two hours. "Nuns
don't walk or bounce, they glide," she chanted
over and over. "Glide! Glide! All expressions of
your outer personality must be submerged in
the part!"

So I glided across the stage until the balls of
my feet hurt. We had to walk with our arms
folded and our hands hidden in the folds of our
sleeves, too, and I was only allowed to show
my hands twice—once when I reached out to

comfort the sobbing Maria, and once when I gestured to the heavens at the end of my song. As nuns, we didn't show our hair, our hands, our feet, or our bodies. A mannequin on roller skates could do it, so why did they need me?

My dinner was in the oven wrapped in foil. "I'm glad you're home," Mom said, coming into the kitchen. "While you're eating, I want to ask you about some things."

I lifted the foil from the plate and looked at my dinner—overdone macaroni and cheese with a wilted sprig of broccoli on the side. Ugh. I took a fork out of the kitchen drawer and pulled a bar stool to the counter. "What, Mom?"

She beamed. "I've gotten four sets of swatches for your dress, honey. I think either green or maroon would be lovely for a Christmas wedding, don't you? With your coloring, do you like the maroon or the deep green?"

She was holding tiny squares of fabric up to my hair and face, and it was hard to eat. "I don't care, Mom," I sighed. "Whatever you think."

"With your dark hair and skin, maybe the maroon is better," she said, comparing two different shades. "Do you like satin or velveteen?"

"Whatever, Mom."

"Satin can look so tacky," she said, thinking aloud. "Maybe with velveteen ribbons in the flowers, a subdued velveteen would be best."

92

I shrugged.

Mom stopped jabbering and looked at me. "You're not very excited about this, are you?"

"I'm just tired, Mom."

She brightened. "OK. Well, get some rest, dear. Have you decided what you're going to sing for our wedding?"

I shook my head.

"Well, when you have, let me know. I'll want to put the name of the song in the program."

She buzzed out of the kitchen, and I took another bite of leathery macaroni. There was one good thing about her getting married: maybe I'd get to eat a decent meal once in a while.

"It's November 12," I told Chip on the telephone, "so put it on your calendar, OK?"

"I wouldn't miss it," he said, and I could hear the pride in his voice. "The singing nun in concert."

"Quit it." It felt good to hear him teasing, though, after a long day like today. "I feel as old as I look with my wrinkles on."

"Wrinkles?"

"Yeah. Miss Cason showed us how they're going to draw wrinkles on most of the nuns. Maria's got to be young, you see, but because we're all the same age in real life, we nuns have got to wear wrinkles. And guess who's the wrinkliest one of all?"

"You, right?"

"Yeah. You don't get to be the Reverend Mother without a *lot* of wrinkles."

We laughed. "Well, Cass, I'd better go," Chip said. "Are you really doing OK? You sound awfully tired."

"Yeah, I'll make it."

"OK. I'll call you soon."

After rehearsal the next night, I was looking forward to going home. I had about an hour's worth of homework, but then I could get to bed early for a change. Rehearsal had been much better today; we nuns were finally getting the hang of gliding and hiding our hands. We'd choreographed the song "How Do You Solve a Problem like Maria?" and it was fun.

I had gathered my books and was about to leave the rehearsal hall when Melissa McMiller stopped me and waved a slip of paper in front of my face.

"Cassie Perkins, a message for you," she said, raising her eyebrow. "What have you done now?"

I snatched the paper from Melissa. "Whatever I did, it's none of your business." But I was scared. What *had* I done?

Nothing. The note was from a secretary in the office who'd taken a phone call from my mother. She wouldn't be able to pick me up because she was still at the dressmaker's. I should catch the bus home.

"Again," I muttered. "I hate taking that old bus."

"Something wrong, Cassie?" It was Shalisa, who walked up and noticed my sour expression.

I shrugged. "It's just that my mother's tied up at her dressmaker's and won't be able to pick me up."

"Does she go to Madame Linda?" Shalisa asked, her eyes sparkling. "My mother gets tied up there for hours sometimes."

I didn't know who Madame Linda was, but I didn't think my mom would be tied up for hours. It was only her wedding dress, and how difficult could that be?

"I'm not sure who she's using," I answered. "She's having her wedding dress fitted."

Shalisa linked her arm through mine. "I know all about it. Of course you know Tom Harris is a member of our club, and he's told my parents all about the wedding. Why don't you come home with me and have dinner with my family? You can call your mom from my house, let her know, and later my dad and I can drive you home."

"I don't know," I argued, but it was useless. Shalisa was practically dragging me down the hall, and frankly, going to a decent meal sounded better than the inevitable peanut butter and jelly sandwich I'd have at home.

"You can't say no," Shalisa said. "My mother will want to meet you and hear all about your family." She squeezed my arm. "I'm so glad we're becoming such good friends!"

12

We sat in the back of the McRay family car, a long black sedan driven by some young guy named Jeffrey. I didn't know who Jeffrey was; he could have been an uncle, a chauffeur, or a friend, but I didn't want to seem stupid and ask.

Shalisa babbled about the dance at the country club where she first met Nick, how lucky I was to have him for a brother, how nice the Harris house was, and how wonderful someone named Louisa was at creating costumes. "Miss Cason was going to have me find my Maria costume from the school's wardrobe department, but I told her Louisa would be able to do much better," Shalisa explained, her hands flying expressively. "Miss Cason agreed immediately. She knows how good Louisa is. Maybe she could even design your costume, Cassie."

"I don't think there's much to a nun's habit,"
I answered, laughing. "By the way, who's
Louisa?"

Shalisa's eyes widened in surprise, then she
laughed delicately. "Why, she's part of the
family. When I was little, she was my nanny,
and now she's sort of our housekeeper." Shalisa
smiled and shrugged her delicate shoulders.
"She's always there when I need her."

I pictured Louisa as a woman like Alice on
the old "Brady Bunch" reruns. A little heavy,
with her hair in a bun, and usually in an apron
and soft-soled shoes. Someone to do the laun-
dry, cook, babysit the kids, and teach them
manners.

"Don't you have a housekeeper?" Shalisa
asked in surprise.

I was embarrassed to admit we didn't. "Not
at my mom's house, because we'll be moving
soon." Then I knew what to say. "But of course,
my dad has Estelle."

"Is she good?"

I rolled my eyes. *"Good* isn't the word. She's
amazing, but she's only been with him for a
short while. We had Bertha before that, but
my dad had to let her go."

Shalisa nodded gravely. "I understand. She
didn't work out?"

I closed my eyes as if the subject were too

painful to talk about. "She was falling apart,"
I whispered. "She just couldn't keep up."

"Oh." That shut Shalisa up long enough
for us to pull into a stunning three-story
Victorian house. Jeffrey drove up the circular
driveway and stopped at the front door. Shalisa
slipped out when he opened the door for us,
and I thanked him as I got out of the car.

"Come on up to my room," Shalisa called,
leading the way. "I'll have Louisa come up, and
maybe she'll braid our hair for dinner. Would
you like a French braid? You can call your mom
from my room, too."

I followed Shalisa blindly, like a little puppy,
through the sparkling white foyer and up a
polished wooden staircase. No wonder the girl
sparkled at everything she did. There wasn't a
speck of dust within miles of here.

Louisa wasn't anything like the Brady Bunch's
Alice. She was about my mother's age, but she
looked young, with long brown hair neatly
pulled back with a headband, and pretty brown
eyes. She was wearing tailored shorts and a
long-sleeved button-down shirt, but she was
professional and polished in everything she did.

She put Shalisa's books away, brushed out her
hair, hung up her clothes, and helped her pick
out something fresh to wear for dinner. She gave
me the telephone, asked if I needed anything,

and, at Shalisa's suggestion, offered to braid my hair.

"No thanks," I said, feeling a little embarrassed. "I'll just leave it the way it is."

"OK," she said, backing out of the room and closing the door. "Just call if you need anything." Imagine! A personal maid. Shalisa probably didn't even know how to make her own bed.

Mom was thrilled when I called and told her where I was. "Of course it's OK, honey," she said. "Tom's told me a lot about the McRays. You enjoy yourself, and I'll expect you home later this evening."

I hung up the phone, and Shalisa looked at me from the reflection in her makeup mirror. "Dinner won't be until seven, so you can study in the library, or we can sit in here and talk," she said, penciling in a fresh coat of lip liner. "Or you can look in my photo albums. There are pictures of our home in the Bahamas and of me with Sylvester Stallone, Beverly Sills, and Tom Hanks."

I picked up a fancy gold album and idly flipped it open. There on the first page was a photograph of Shalisa surrounded by the Boys of the Band, the hottest new rock group of the year.

"I can't believe this," I gasped. "Where did you see the Boys?"

"Oh—" Shalisa smacked her lips together to smooth out her lipstick. "Daddy hired them last year to play at my birthday party. It was very hush-hush. You wouldn't believe the mobs of girls who knew they were in town but didn't know where." She giggled. "All the time they were right down the hall in our guest rooms."

I was beginning to feel uncomfortable. What was I doing here? Shalisa lived in some crazy world where celebrities stopped by for dinner and pop stars sang at birthday parties. She had a maid, a chauffeur, and a wing of guest rooms. She didn't need a friend like me.

"Are you sure I should stay for dinner?" I asked, watching Shalisa pull on a black cashmere sweater. "I feel kind of grungy after the long day at school."

"Don't worry about it." Shalisa smiled. "It's just a simple family dinner. Look at me—I'm even wearing jeans."

I followed Shalisa down to the dining room, but almost turned and ran when I saw the spread on the dining room table. There were four chairs—for Shalisa, me, and her mom and dad—but the food wasn't on the table. It was in long silver dishes on a buffet table. The table was covered in shining silver, crystal goblets, and four or five dishes for each place.

At home I would have eaten on my orange plastic plate (found free in giant bags of Suki's dog food) and drunk from one of the mismatched glasses that Dad didn't take when he moved out.

This was a simple family dinner? Shalisa pulled out a chair and motioned for me to take the one across from her, so we sat down and waited for her parents to arrive.

Right on the stroke of seven, Mr. and Mrs. Steven McRay came in. I remembered my manners and stood up. Mr. McRay shook my hand when Shalisa introduced me, and Mrs. McRay smiled and said she would have to invite my mother for lunch one day soon.

We sat down and Jeffrey and Louisa came in to serve us. They brought the dishes of food from the buffet table to us and actually put the food on our plates. It was kind of embarrassing, like we couldn't even dish out our own food. But at least I knew Mom would be pleased that I hadn't made a fool out of myself. I did whatever Shalisa did—unfolded my napkin when she did, put it in my lap like she did, and even drank a sip of water when she did.

Mr. McRay ate without speaking, and I noticed he emptied his wine glass three or four times, with Jeffrey always there to fill it again. Mrs. McRay babbled pleasantly about things at the country club, the current political situation, and when she and Shalisa would ever find the time to do their extensive Christmas shopping.

There was a lull in the conversation, and I tried to think of something to say. I decided to give Mrs. McRay a compliment. "Those are lovely roses," I said, nodding my head toward the arrangement of roses in the center of the table. "Red roses are my favorite flowers."

Mrs. McRay seemed surprised, as if she hadn't even noticed them. "They are lovely, aren't they?" she said, glancing over at the flowers. She seemed to soften, and her eyes even got a little watery. "They must have come from the rose garden. I used to work out there myself, planting and pruning, but I just don't have time anymore."

"Really, Mother," Shalisa chided gently. "Why should you work in the yard? That's why we have a gardener."

"I suppose." Mrs. McRay stopped looking at the flowers and studied her plate. "But I have such fond memories of those days."

Louisa and Jeffrey cleared our plates and brought out dessert, a luscious chocolate pie. After the dessert had been served, Mrs. McRay turned to me. "I'm not familiar with the Perkins family," she said, as if apologizing. "Are your parents from here, dear?"

I shook my head. "My dad was from Ohio, and my mom was born in Washington state," I explained. "They met when Dad was in college."

"From where do you get your lovely black hair?"

I laughed. "My dad's mother was named Caparelli," I explained. "We're Italian. Grand-mother immigrated when Dad was a little boy."

"Oh." Mrs. McRay leaned back in her chair and frowned slightly. "And what did you say your father does? Is he a boxer, or is he in one of those Italian crime families?" She shuddered slightly. "No wonder your lovely mother kicked him out."

I could feel the blood rushing to my face. "My father is a wonderful man," I said. "He's a systems analyst at NASA. He's very smart. My brother is a genius. My mother is a very talented interior decorator, and she didn't kick my father out."

"I see." Mrs. McRay didn't say anything else, she just put her spoon on the edge of her dessert plate so Louisa could quickly whisk it away.

I looked around at them. Was this a normal family? Was this what I'd be getting when Mom married Tom Harris? Would Tom be at one end of the table, more interested in his wine glass than in the people around him, and would Mom turn into a snotty country-clubber at the other end? Would Nick and I just sit there while Uncle Jacob did all the work?

The worst part of it all was that Shalisa just sat there, as calm and collected as ever. She hadn't even noticed that her mother had insulted my father because she was too busy telling Louisa all about the play, as if Louisa really cared, which I was sure she didn't.

I decided it was time to strike a blow for normal families everywhere. This family needed shaking up, and if they ended up not liking me anymore, it would still be worth it.

"My brother," I said loudly, to get everyone's attention, "is a genius, that's true. But he might be a genius because he has epilepsy. He gets seizures sometimes."

"How awful!" Mrs. McRay said, covering her hand with her napkin.

"Yes," I said, nodding. "Once he fell into the river, and I pulled him out. He was covered in mud, lying there twitching, and I had to try to give him mouth-to-mouth resus—"

"Cassie," Shalisa interrupted, listening now. "Can we talk about this later?"

Mr. McRay's eyes had lost their glassy look, and he was looking at me in amazement. I don't think he would have been any more surprised if my chair had suddenly begun to talk.

"Would you like to talk about Estelle?" I asked. "You said you wanted to hear about my family, and this is all real-life stuff."

Shalisa nodded and smiled at her mother. "Estelle is their new maid," she explained.

Mr. McRay took another sip of wine.

"Well, she's not really a maid," I said. "She's more of a chauffeur. Dad picked her out because she's hot-looking." I winked at Mrs. McRay. "He said because he was divorced, he didn't need the family-man image anymore. You should see him and Estelle driving around town! Max goes with them, sometimes—" I shook my head. "Although three is definitely a crowd."

Mr. McRay spewed wine out of his mouth and nearly choked, while Mrs. McRay went white. Shalisa's mouth was open.

"Your father thinks this is respectable?" Mrs. McRay asked, her eyes wide.

I shrugged. "Why not? He says Estelle makes him feel younger or something."

Mrs. McRay glared at Shalisa then, and I could see clearly a where-did-you-get-this-girl message in her eyes.

"Well, you wanted to know about my family," I said, pushing my chair back and standing up. "If there's anything else you want to know, just ask."

I was almost out the door, but I remembered one thing. "Oh, I don't have a way home now," I said. "Should I call my dad and ask him to bring Estelle?"

"Jeffrey, please take the young lady home," Mrs. McRay said, hiding her face behind her napkin. "Right away."

As I left the dining room, I overheard Mrs. McRay say, "Poor Tom Harris must be crazy to marry into that family! Do you think he'll send that horrid girl off to boarding school?"

I looked up at Jeffrey as we walked out to the car. "Do you like sports cars, Jeffrey?"

"Yeah, I do."

"You'd like Estelle. Dad says she's the sweetest convertible on the road today."

"Really?" He opened the sedan's door for me. "How fast does she go?"

I smiled and climbed in. "Zero to sixty in 5.5 seconds. Fast enough to leave this crowd in the dust."

Jeffrey grinned. "That's fast enough."

13

If I had embarrassed Andrea in front of her parents, she would have thrown a royal temper tantrum and been mad at me for days, maybe even weeks. But Shalisa was different. After that disastrous dinner at her house, she avoided me for a couple of days, then she began going out of her way to treat me nicely. With pity. As if I were mentally ill or something.

Word must have gotten around that Cassie Perkins was unstable (or that my father was doing an unpardonable thing like riding around town with his beautiful chauffeur) because all of a sudden no one would talk to me. I always had a table to myself at lunch, and in rehearsals everyone avoided me. I didn't care. I was going to be out of this school in seven months, anyway.

Even the teachers left me alone. Mr. Granger

stopped picking on me and began ignoring me altogether. Mr. Levy walked around me in dance class as if I didn't exist, and Miss Cason let me read my lines only when she absolutely had to. Only Mrs. Blackwelder believed in me. During voice lessons, I'd sing, and she'd close her eyes and say, "Yes, Cassie, sing from your soul! You've got the song inside you, so let it out so others may hear it!"

No one else wanted to hear it. I had the distinct impression that I was walking a tightrope. I didn't fit in here at the Spa, and if I weren't Tom Harris's soon-to-be stepdaughter, I'd probably be out already. As it was, I knew if I rocked the boat even one more time, I'd be out of the play, and I didn't want to lose that. I only came to this school because I wanted to perform.

When I came home on Friday afternoon, I nearly walked smack into a huge For Sale sign in our front yard. I was stunned. I mean, it was one thing to talk about moving, but it was something else to see a huge sign advertising that your life was in turmoil. Without thinking, I pulled the sign up out of the soft dirt and dragged it over to the side of the house where we kept our garbage cans. There! Now Andrea wouldn't drive by and be upset.

It was Max's weekend to come to our house, and I couldn't wait to see him. I was dying to tell him all about my episode at the McRays, but at six o'clock, Max still hadn't shown up.

Mom came in, though, her arms loaded with wallpaper books.

"Where's Max?" I asked. "He's late."

"What?" She unloaded the books onto the kitchen counter. "No 'Hello, Mom?'"

I rolled my eyes. "Hello. Why isn't Max here? I'm worried."

"It's OK." She took her purse off her shoulder and tossed it onto the counter, too. "I canceled Max's weekend here because you and I will be at the Harrises' house most of the time. I figured since Max wouldn't be living there, there wouldn't be any sense in having him wander around. He'd only be miserable."

I sank onto a stool. She canceled Max's weekend? We'd be at the Harrises'? What was going on?

Mom caught her breath and explained. "Tom wants me to redecorate his house since we girls will be moving in. Do you realize it's less than two months now until the big move? I looked the house over today, and I really think we'll only have to redo the master bedroom, the den, the dining room, and, of course, your room, Cassie. I want you to take a look at it and let me know what you'd like."

She smiled, totally happy. "We'll go over first thing in the morning, have lunch and dinner there, and be home probably late tomorrow night. On Sunday we'll catch up with anything we miss the first time through. Isn't this going to be fun?"

She reached up to pat my cheek, but I turned my head. I think I might have hurt her feelings a little, but she just ignored me and reached for the mail.

"Hmmm, there's a brochure in here about the Reeding Hills Boarding School for Girls," she said, pulling out the brochure. "Did you send for this, Cass?"

"No." I shook my head. "But you might have Tom ask Mrs. McRay about it."

"Boarding school?" Mom took the mail and walked off toward her room. "Why would I send my kid to boarding school?"

"You won't have to," I whispered under my breath. "I'll go live with Dad first."

The phone rang at about eight o'clock and I jumped for it, hoping to hear from either Chip or Andrea. I was so busy during the week I didn't have any time to hear from my real friends anymore. But it was Max on the phone.

"Hi, Whiz Kid," I teased him. "I hear you get the weekend off. Lucky you." Max didn't answer, but I heard a sniff on the phone. "Max? Are you all right?"

112

There was more sniffling, then a weak, "Yeah. I guess so."

"Max, what's wrong?" I cupped my hand over the phone so my voice wouldn't carry into the living room where Mom was bent over wallpaper books. "Did one of your gerbils die? Did something happen at school? Is Dad OK? Did you get sick?"

"Nothing like that," Max answered, his voice a little stronger now. "And Dad's fine; he's out getting groceries. I've just been thinking. Mom's getting married, and you two are moving, and Tom has a kid . . ." Max hesitated.

"So?"

"She didn't want me around this weekend because you're going to Tom's house."

I didn't see the connection. "She thought you'd be bored, Max."

Max was quiet for a minute. "I think she wants to forget me," he finally whispered. "She's going to get married and forget all about me."

All that was hidden in Max came out in angry, broken sobbing. I didn't know what to do. I wanted to hug him, but I couldn't. He was sitting alone in Dad's house, crying on the phone, and breaking my heart.

Didn't Mom realize what she had done? "Max, it'll be OK," I whispered. "Come on, stop crying. Mom's not going to forget you. She loves you."

"It . . . won't . . . be . . . the same," Max sobbed, his words coming out slowly, painfully.

I was worried about Max. Not only was he upset, but if he got too tired and upset, he might have a seizure, and he was all alone in the house. What if he fell and hit his head?

"Max, you've got to calm down," I told him. "Take a deep breath. Remember, you're too smart to let something like this throw you. Your mother loves you. She cannot forget you. You think she can forget the kid who invented Fido's Fricassee?"

Max stopped sniffling.

"You think she can forget the kid who blew up the garage when he was five years old?"

He sighed.

"You think she can forget the kid who hid an alligator in the bathtub for a week?"

Finally, he gave a weak laugh.

"Max, you've got to trust Mom. I've got to trust Mom. And more than that, we've got to trust God."

I'd never told Max about giving my life to Jesus. Somehow it had never come up, and we didn't spend nearly as much time together as we used to.

"Trust God?"

"Yeah. That he loves us and will work out a plan for us. And when everything's going wrong, we can still trust his plan."

"I don't know, Cass. I'm not sure I can believe in a supernatural God."

"Then for now, Max, trust me. I know he's there."

"Can you prove it?" Max the scientist was talking now.

"Not now. But I believe in him. And I think I ought to trust him. There's sure no one else around to trust."

Max grunted. "You're right about that." He paused. "But I can't believe in something without proof."

"You're the genius, you work it out. All I know is I believe in God, and I trust him."

14

I meant to call Chip or Doug Richlett and ask how I could prove God to Max, but I got all caught up in Mom's plans for the Harris house, or, as she kept calling it, "our new house."

On Saturday morning she loaded her swatches, her notebooks, and an armload of wallpaper books into the car. I stood at the door, gloomily watching rain clouds gather overhead. Suki wanted to come along and ran out the door before I could stop her. "Can't she go?" I asked Mom. "It's going to be her new house, too."

"Not today, Cass," Mom called, standing by the car with her palm pressed against her forehead. "I feel as though I'm forgetting something."

I put Suki back in the house and got into the car, sulking a little. Finally Mom snapped her fingers. "The real estate agent was supposed to be by here and put out our For Sale sign! I can't believe she hasn't been by!"

I thought about not mentioning it, but something inside told me I should confess. I had promised God I wouldn't make things worse, so I scrunched up my face and stuck my head out the car window. "The sign's over by the garbage cans," I said quietly. "I just wasn't ready to see it up yet, so I took it down."

Mom gave me a blank look, then she slowly rocked back and forth on her heels, debating whether or not she should put the sign back up. Finally she walked around the car and got in. "It won't matter if we put it up on Monday," she said, smiling. "It is kind of sad to think about leaving this old house, isn't it?"

She started the car, and I looked at the house as we pulled out of the driveway. I had learned to ride my bike on this driveway, and Max had found his favorite garter snake in the rose bushes that divided our lawn from Mr. Bushnell's. The front window was where Max and I had stood when Dad left the house and drove away for good. Now Mom and I were driving away, and soon we'd be staying away, too.

Mom was listening to the radio and not talking, and I was glad. There was a big lump in my throat, and I couldn't talk if I'd tried.

The Harris house wasn't as imposing as

Shalisa's, but it was in a very nice neighborhood and still made our house look dinky. It was a two-story house in a Swiss chalet style, and I had been there once before to visit Nick. Back then I never dreamed I'd soon be moving in as Nick's stepsister.

Tom Harris must have been waiting for us, because as soon as Mom slammed her car door, he opened the front door and was marching toward us. "The day is all yours, and so is the house," he said, smiling and slipping an arm around her. "Cassie, we want you to feel at home, too. I'll do anything to please my two girls."

Gag. I couldn't help making a face, so I turned my head so Mom wouldn't see. Mom might be "his girl," but I would never be.

"Is Uncle Jacob home?" I asked, leaving them on the lawn.

"He's in the library," Tom called. "Make yourself at home."

I liked Uncle Jacob the first time I met him because he didn't pretend to be anything. He was gruff and loud and sort of a slob sometimes, but I didn't care.

I found him bent over an ancient-looking typewriter with his customary cigar stuck in his mouth. "Haven't you traded that thing in yet for a pacifier?" I teased. "Or at least a lollipop? That's so gross!"

"Why, it's my Cassie songbird." Uncle Jacob stopped pounding the keys and grinned at me, the tip of the never-lit cigar bobbing up and down. "And no, since I gave up smoking these things, I just can't write without one in my mouth. Old habits die hard, ya know."

I sank onto a leather sofa in front of his typing table. "We're decorating this place," I said with a shrug. "So here I am."

"Aye, so ya are. And what am I supposed to do with you underfoot all day, in my way, making a mess of the place?"

"I won't be in the way." I leaned over and turned one of his typed pages so I could read it. "Working on this week's column for the newspaper?"

"Yep." He pounded a few more keys. "It's about apathy. People just don't care about things anymore, and they're letting things slide."

"Like what things?"

Uncle Jacob scowled at me. "I thought you said you wouldn't be in the way. How can I write if you're asking me questions all the time? Go up and help your mama decorate your new room."

"I don't want to."

"Why not?"

"Because I don't care anything about it."

Uncle Jacob snapped his fingers in my face.

"That's apathy. Cassie, my girl, I never thought I'd hear it from you."

I leaned back on the couch and shrugged. "Why should I care? Nobody cares about what I think, so caring is just a waste of energy."

"Not true," Uncle Jacob said, still pounding the keys. He ripped the page out of his typewriter and swept it up with the others on his desk. "Done. Well, if you don't care about your room, do you care about what you'll be eatin' for lunch?"

I couldn't stop a grin. "I guess I do."

"Come on, then." He stood up and led the way into the kitchen. "Let's get the kettle on the stove."

I felt a strange sense of deja vu in the dining room. Tom Harris was at one end of the long table, and Mom was at the other. Nick sat on one side of the table, and there was an empty place for me across from Nick. The Harrises didn't have a maid, but Uncle Jacob and I were busy bringing in steaming bowls and dishes from the kitchen. Maybe Tom Harris thought I'd be a good maid.

When everything was in, Tom told me to have a seat. I sat down, feeling almost guilty. Was I supposed to help, or wasn't I? Here I was, trying to fit into a rich family, and I didn't know all the rules.

Uncle Jacob came back in with a coffeepot, and I waited for Tom to tell us to eat. But instead the silence was broken by a bellow from Uncle Jacob. "What in tarnation?" he thundered. "Where am I supposed to sit?"

Tom Harris looked guilty then, and he jumped up. "Sorry, Jake," he apologized, smiling sheepishly. "Let me bring in a chair."

The corner of Uncle Jacob's mouth turned up, and I laughed. Maybe this family wasn't going to be like the McRays, after all. Tom was out scampering for a chair, and Mom had already begun to pass bowls of food. Nick was grabbing fried chicken with his fingers, as messy as Max could ever be.

Uncle Jacob took the chair Tom offered and pulled it over next to me. He raised an eyebrow. "Aren't you going to move your chair, missy?" he said, as if insulted.

"Of course." I slipped my chair down a few inches. "But you don't have a plate or silverware."

Uncle Jacob looked pointedly across the table at Nick. "I cooked your lunch, young man," he said sternly, "and it was your job to set the table. Did you forget how to add three plus two?"

"Sorry, Uncle Jake," Nick said, red-faced. He slipped out of his chair and returned from the kitchen in a few minutes with a plate and silverware for Uncle Jacob.

I was a little relieved. As long as Uncle Jacob was around, everything just might be all right.

After lunch, Mom insisted on showing me my new room. It was upstairs and in the right front corner of the house. From the window I could look out through the branches of an old oak tree and see the street. Nice for spying, I thought, if I ever need to.

Tom had emptied the room completely and had all the walls painted white. The floor was covered in a pretty pink-patterned carpet. "How should we do it?" Mom asked. "I thought you'd want to bring your antique bedroom suite from home, but we can wallpaper or paint, and get new curtains and a bedspread. What do you want to do, honey?"

I had been looking out the window, and I really didn't want to think about this room. It was obvious that Mom wanted to really decorate it, and not just hand it over to me. My old room was covered in posters and pictures I'd had since I was six, and one whole wall was devoted to shelves containing my collection of little green ceramic frogs.

"Well, I don't know, Mom," I said, turning away from the window. "By the time we bring over my posters and my frog shelves and my bed and dresser, I don't know that we'll need to do anything. I'll just cover the walls with stuff."

Mom sat down on the carpet next to a wall-

paper book titled *Sweet and Delicate Prints*.
"Cass, you're growing up, and I think this is
a good time for you to leave a lot of that imma-
ture stuff behind," she said, carefully choosing
her words. "You don't want to keep your bronze
baby shoes out forever, do you? And those
frogs . . . ," she laughed. "Honey, you can't
keep stuff like that forever."

I pulled my chin up and looked away.

"And, Cassie, you can see that this house
isn't like our other house. We rarely entertained
over there, and no one ever went into your
room except Max and Andrea. But here, honey,
Tom will be entertaining clients, and people
may want to use your room for changing, or
for leaving their coats, or . . . ," her voice trailed
off. "I'll bet your friend Shalisa's room wasn't
cluttered with stuff."

I remembered Shalisa's elegant room: white
carpet, billowing white curtains, white bed
curtains hanging from the ceiling. White wicker
furniture, even a white bearskin rug or something on the floor. "Shalisa's not normal," I
muttered. "I just want to be myself."

"You can keep that stuff, honey, if you want
to," Mom said. "But just keep it out of sight,
in a closet or a box. We can keep everything
in the attic, and you can visit your stuff whenever you want. Now come on, what color do

you want? Anything, honey, just tell me something."

She was trying hard, but I wasn't in the mood. "OK," I said, turning back to look at her. "I want black. Black curtains and black paint. Black furniture. I'm in mourning, and I want black. You can even recover Suki's little bed in black."

Mom was angry now. "That's enough, Cass. Now be serious and tell me something reasonable, or I'll choose something myself. You can't live here in a black room. And about Suki," she said, taking a deep breath, "you're going to have to talk to Tom about her. I don't think he wants a dog."

"Then I'll live at Dad's place," I snapped, forgetting all my good intentions. "I'll call him tonight and let him know I'm coming. You can go to court and tell the judge whatever you have to to work it out. Max thinks you've forgotten about him anyhow—well, I'll go too and spare you the problem of sending me to boarding school. You can live here in this nice, white, clean house without dogs or mess or real kids, and Max and Dad and I will be a normal family. We will do quite nicely even if we never see you again!"

I stomped down the stairs and didn't look back, but I couldn't help hearing a loud, choking sound from Mom. I had hurt her. Fine. Let her hurt for a while. I was tired of hurting, and I wasn't going to do it anymore.

Remember this—if you're ever planning to throw a tantrum, make sure you've got someplace to go when you're done. That was my mistake at the Harris house. It wasn't my house, and there wasn't anyplace I could go to sit and just be mad for a while. Uncle Jacob was in the library, and I knew he'd set me straight, and I'd have to listen, so I couldn't go there. Nick was out by the pool, and he was a know-nothing, so I couldn't go there. Tom was puttering around downstairs, and I despised him, so I wasn't safe there. Mom was sitting upstairs, crying in the hall, and I couldn't go back there, either. I'd only end up crying, too, and saying I was sorry. I wasn't ready to do that yet.

So I marched straight out the front door and let it slam. Ordinarily I'd have called Suki and taken her for a walk, telling her everything until I had gotten it all out of my system. But Suki wasn't allowed in this spotless house.

But it helped to think about her as I walked. I thought about the day Dad took Max and me to pick her up. She was a Christmas present from Dad, just a tiny thing, small enough to fit into the palm of Dad's hand. I was little, too, only five years old.

"Pugs are one-man dogs," the lady with the

puppies had said. "They like everyone, but they'll pick one special person to love."

Oh, how I had wanted that little dog to love me. Mom was busy, Dad worked all the time, and even though Max was little more than a baby, he was already proving himself to be a genius. He was carrying on conversations before he could walk, so he sure didn't need anyone. But I did.

By some miracle, it was me who Suki loved. She began sleeping in my bed as soon as Mom was sure she was properly trained, and her two favorite places for sleeping were either at my feet or on my pillow. As she grew bigger, I had to get an extra pillow so Suki would have enough room. In the middle of the night sometimes, she'd wake me up, snoring in my ear. But it was nice having her head next to mine.

As I walked quickly down the street, my anger slowly fading, I remembered another time I'd rushed down a sidewalk. I was about nine, and Mom had forgotten and left Suki out in the yard one day while I was at school. Someone, probably an electric company meter reader, had left our gate open. When I got home, Suki wasn't there to greet me, and I knew something terrible had happened.

Pugs are known for their pushed-in noses, but believe me, those noses aren't very good at smelling things. I was afraid Suki was lost and wouldn't be able to sniff her way back home. Max and I both took off on foot, and we looked for an hour without finding her. Mom came home then, and she felt guilty enough about leaving Suki outside that she took us to look for Suki in the station wagon. We sat in the back with the window open as Mom drove slowly up and down the streets in our neighborhood. We whistled and called until we were hoarse.

We had to go home when it got dark, but we hadn't seen Suki anywhere. Dad had come home while we were out, and he opened the door for us. "There you are!" he said. "Why did you go off and leave Suki waiting by the door?" I thought I'd burst with happiness. Max was glad, too, and Mom cried from sheer relief.

I stopped walking, remembering how splotchy Mom's face looked when she was crying. She was crying now because of me, just like that day years ago.

I turned around and walked back.

15

When I came in, Uncle Jacob stood in the foyer and pointed wordlessly toward Mom and Tom in the living room. I knew they'd be waiting for me.

"You understand that where you live is not your decision, it's your father's and mine," Mom said, looking at me through red-rimmed eyes.

I sat on the couch and looked down at my chewed-up fingernails. "I know."

"And Cassie, I want you with me," Mom said, her eyes filling with tears again.

Tom took over. "Your mother knows this is a time of transition for you, and things aren't always easy," he said. (Was that the understatement of the year!) "But she hasn't stopped loving you."

"And we're not sending you to boarding school," Mom said, shaking her head. "I don't know where you got that idea. And if Max is upset, well, I'll talk to him and straighten things out. But you two are still my children, and I will always love you."

Tom walked over to where Mom stood by the fireplace and slipped his arm around her. "I think maybe you and I should get to know one another, Cass," he said. "Why don't I pick you up tomorrow, and we can spend some time together."

It wasn't a question, so I knew I had to go. It was a sentence: *You, Cassie Perkins, are hereby sentenced to spending several hours in the company of Tom Harris for the crime of making your mother cry.* It was a stiff penalty, but I probably deserved it.

I wanted to go to church with Chip on Sunday morning, but Mom got me up early and reminded me that Tom would be by to pick me up at nine-thirty. "I think he's taking you to the Country Inn for breakfast," she said, smiling a little too brightly. "You'll love it. That's one of my favorite places."

I wanted to crawl back under my quilt and hide, but Suki looked up at me with her buggy brown eyes and barked softly. She had to go out, so I walked her to the back door and let her out in the yard.

Suki and I were both a little surprised when we got outside. It was going to be a cool day. Fall came late to Florida, when it came at all, and

130

today there was a slight nip in the air. It would probably be broiling hot by lunchtime, but I could probably wear a sweater to breakfast without sweating to death.

So at least I looked nice when Tom rang the doorbell. Mom let him in, and when I came into the living room, he was standing there as cool as ever in his golf shirt and slacks. His hair was perfect even on the weekend, combed over to the side, and thick. My Dad would probably have given even little red Estelle to have thick hair like Tom's. Tom was holding a red rose.

"For you," he said, offering it to me. "I always give roses to very special ladies."

I bit my lip, hoping Mom hadn't heard. She'd wonder why he sent daisies for her birthday.

"Thanks," I said, taking the rose and tossing it onto the coffee table. He could bring a whole basket of roses, for all I cared. Roses weren't going to win me over.

"Are you ready?" Tom asked.

I nodded and was out the door before he could say anything else. I heard him coming after me, though, and he followed me to the passenger side of his Mercedes as if to open my door for me. I yanked the door open, hopped in, and slammed the door before he could say anything.

Mom was outside, too, and I caught her rolling her eyes in my direction. She murmured something to Tom, and he answered in a low voice I couldn't hear. Then he got in the car with me and we drove away.

In the restaurant, I ordered the most expensive thing on the menu. "I'll have the Hungry Man's breakfast tray," I told our waitress. "Plus a side order of grapefruit, a Danish roll, hot chocolate, and sausage biscuits and gravy."

The waitress raised her eyebrow, but Tom smiled and handed her his menu. "I'll just have a fruit plate," he said, "and hot coffee."

She took our menus and left, and Tom looked at me. "Hungry?"

I wasn't really, but if he was going to insist on taking me to breakfast, then he was going to pay for it. *Really* pay for it.

I shrugged. "My mom's a horrible cook, so when I have a chance to eat out, I eat."

"Yes, I know that about your mother," Tom said, smiling. "But she's so many other wonderful things I don't care about her cooking."

I shrugged again and blew a bubble with my gum. Tom stared at it until it popped and I started chewing again.

"Cass, I wanted us to have some time together—" he began, but I interrupted.

"Cassie," I said. "Only Mom and Max call me Cass."

Tom nodded and shifted back in his seat. "OK, Cassie. What I want you to know is that

I'm going to be good to your mother and fair with you. Even if you can't love me—"

I made a face. I couldn't help it.

"Or even *like* me, I still think you can learn to respect me."

My gum snapped loudly.

Tom folded his arms. "The thing is, you and your mother won't have to worry any more about the house or how you're going to pay the bills. I'm going to take care of both of you. I'll pay your tuition wherever you want to go to school and support you like you were my own daughter. If anything ever happened to your dad, I'd even adopt you. You'd be Cassie Harris."

I stopped chewing and stared at him. "I don't *want* to be Cassie Harris," I said flatly. "Not ever. I'm not your daughter, and I never will be. OK?"

Tom put his hands up in midair as if surrendering. "OK. I won't force anything on you that you don't want. But you've got to do your part, too. You'll have to obey the house rules as long as you live in our house, and I want your respect. No sassing, no running away, and no more outbursts. I don't want your mother hurt."

Who was going to keep *me* from getting hurt? But as I sat there, looking at Tom Harris, I thought he at least looked sincere. He really did care about my mother, and he really hadn't ever done anything to actually hurt me, Mom, or Max. Besides, he was pretty brave, taking me out for breakfast where I could have thrown a royal tantrum and embarrassed him to death in public.

OK. I'd respect him a little. Until he blew it. I nodded. "That's fair."

"Good." He smiled at me as the waitress brought his coffee cup. "I know Nick is looking forward to having you around. Max, too, when he comes for the weekends."

I blew another bubble, and when it popped, I told him: "I switched the flowers, you know."

"What?"

"The time you sent Mom roses for her birthday. I put your card on a dinky little bouquet that Dad sent for Max."

He was bewildered for a minute, then his face broke out into a grin. "You sly thing! Did you ever tell your mom?"

I shook my head. "No. Right after that I promised God I wouldn't meddle anymore."

"Well?" He poured cream into his coffee. "Did she like the dinky bouquet?"

I couldn't help smiling. "Yeah. A lot better than the roses. She gave them away."

Tom laughed then, and the people in the next booth looked over to see what was so funny.

"You're something else, Cass, I mean, Cassie," he said, stirring his cup. "There's just one other thing I want to talk to you about."

134

Uh oh. A warning flashed in my head.

"I have an allergy to dogs," Tom said. "I like dogs, but when I'm around them my nose runs, and I'm pretty miserable. Your mom said maybe it would be better if you let Suki live with your dad. That way you could visit her every other weekend."

I shook my head. "You don't understand. Suki's my dog. She's attached to me. If Suki doesn't move, then I don't move."

"Come on now." Tom looked at me as if I were a five-year-old begging for a toy I couldn't have. "Be reasonable, Cassie. Surely that old dog can't mean that much to you?"

"Suki's been in my life for eight years," I explained slowly. "Max has only been around for ten. Therefore, I love Suki almost as much as I love Max. She's part of the family, and you're marrying her, too."

Tom looked for a minute like he'd be happy to divorce at least me and Suki, but he threw his hands up again and gave up. "OK, I'll let you win on this one," he said, forcing a smile. "If there's one thing I've learned as a lawyer, it's the art of compromise. But you owe me one, OK?"

I didn't know what he meant, but I nodded. "I'll keep her in my room," I promised. "That can be house rule number one. Why don't you tell me the others so I won't make any mistakes?"

16

Andrea came over that afternoon. "I saw the
For Sale sign the other day," she sighed. "I can't
believe you're moving away, Cassie."

"It isn't that far," I said, stretching out on the
floor of my room. "And in two years, you can
drive over to see me."

"It'll be forever until I can drive," Andrea
said, plopping down on my bed. She looked
around at my room. "So you can't take all this
neat stuff, huh?"

"No," I said as I rolled over onto my stomach
and buried my face in the old familiar carpet.
"Unless I keep it in a box. It isn't cultured."

"That's too bad." Andrea looked around. "Can
I have your posters? I'll just keep them for you,
and you can come over and see them in *my* room."

I turned my head toward her. "Yeah. You can
have them all. You can even have Mr. Willie."

Andrea smiled, then looked down at me. "Honestly, Cassie, a lot of kids would be thrilled to be moving into a big house in a rich neighborhood. Why are you so depressed?"

"You don't understand." I flopped back over on my back, as limp as a beached whale. Suki snuggled next to me for her afternoon nap. "Tom Harris doesn't know anything about us, at least, not about me or Max. All he knows is what Mom has told him, and who knows what that is?"

I sighed. "He doesn't know anything about when we were little kids, he's never done anything with us, and he doesn't even live like we do. And in less than a month, we're moving into his house, and he thinks we're supposed to be happy about being a part of his family."

Andrea nodded slowly. "I think I understand," she said. "At least I'm trying to."

"And the Harris house has all these weird rules. No touching the pool table because the acid from your hands might eat away the felt. No opening the door to his display cabinets in the library. No reading his law books or bending his baseball cards. No eating from his private cupboard in the kitchen."

"A private cupboard?" Andrea laughed. "What's in it?"

"Nuts. He has these special nuts from Hawaii, macadamia nuts, and no one's allowed to touch them but Tom and Mom." I groaned. "It even rhymes."

"What else?"

"He swims laps in the pool at night, and he's not used to having women around, so I'm not supposed to go out to the pool at night unless I'm *sure* he's not out there."

"Why would he care about that?"

"Because he said he doesn't always wear a bathing suit."

"Ugh!" Andrea squealed in disgust.

"Exactly." I looked up at the ceiling. "And Uncle Jacob runs the house, so he will give me and Nick chores to do, and we're supposed to do them. It's going to be *so* weird."

"I guess."

We were quiet for a few minutes, the kind of quiet that good friends fall into and don't feel awkward. Finally I looked up. *"The Sound of Music's* in two weeks, you know."

"I know. I'm coming, even if all you do is glide around in a long black dress."

I giggled. "Thanks. Chip is coming, too, so at least I'll have two friends in the audience."

"What about the wedding?"

"I'm not wearing a long black dress. I'm gliding around in a long maroon dress."

"Not that, silly. I mean, are you going to invite me to the wedding?"

I looked up at her. "You haven't gotten an invitation yet?"

"No."

"Well, I'm sure you will." I studied the ceiling

of my room. "That's all Mom can think about—invitations, flowers, clothes, and food. I'm sure you'll be hearing from her soon."

The days before our performance of *The Sound of Music* went by in a whirl. I studied, practiced, sang, and danced every day until I thought my head, lips, and legs would fall off. Everyone seemed to be happy. Tom Harris thought he had made his peace with me, Mom was preoccupied with wedding preparations, Max spent his weekend with us with his nose in a book, and Dad stayed out of the way.

One night Tom was taking Mom out to dinner, and I caught him alone in our living room. "Can we talk?" I asked, knowing Mom wasn't ready yet.

"Sure, Cassie," he said, propping up a pillow on the couch as if I were supposed to sit next to him. "What's up?"

I sat in my favorite wing chair, another piece of my life that wasn't moving to the Harris house. "You gave me a long list of house rules the other day, remember?"

He nodded. "Yes, and you agreed they were reasonable, right?"

I nodded, too. "But you didn't ask if there are any rules *you* should know about."

Tom smiled. "OK, what should I know?"

I cleared my throat and pulled out a list I'd been putting together all week. "One: Suki is old and fragile and can't take the heat. We never leave her outside more than ten minutes at a time."

Tom raised a warning finger. "I thought we agreed that the dog was your responsibility anyway. Don't worry, no one in my family—I mean, Nick or Uncle Jacob—will bother your dog. What's next?"

I looked at my list. "Max likes to dress up in costumes while he's working on his experiments. We don't tease him about it."

Tom nodded seriously. "OK. No teasing."

"Number three: we don't have to call you Dad."

Tom's eyes looked pretty serious, but he nodded. "OK, not if you don't want to."

"Number four: never call me Cassiopeia."

"OK."

"Number five: never laugh or say anything bad about my father."

He nodded. "OK. I'll remember."

"And number six: if you marry my mother, never divorce her."

Tom looked down at the carpet. "Does your mother know about these rules?"

"No." I shifted in my chair. "She doesn't."

"OK, I promise to honor each of them." He looked up at me and extended his hand. "Shall we shake on it?"

"We don't have to," I said, getting up and turning away. "If I can't trust a lawyer, who can I trust?"

17

It was the evening of November 12, and
Shalisa McRay was walking around backstage
with her arms full of long-stemmed white
roses. "Aren't they delicious?" she asked as I
passed. "They're from Miss Cason and the other
faculty members." She grabbed my hand and
whispered in my ear. "Your turn will come,
Cassie."

I shook her hand off, but forced a smile. "I
know," I said simply. "I'm going to take my turn
tonight."

I walked off before she could ask what I meant,
but I didn't want to explain. There was no
way I could possibly steal the show while wearing a long black robe and two dozen eyebrow-
pencilled wrinkles, but I really wanted to do my
best.

The performance hall was crowded with

friends, parents, and patrons of the School for the Performing Arts. The curtain went up, and Shalisa was stunning as the young Maria, singing in the mountain meadow. It was going to be a good show.

During our first nuns' number, "How Do You Solve a Problem like Maria," I sneaked a few glances at the audience. Tom and Mom, Nick, and Uncle Jacob were down front, in the special VIP seats. Dad and Max were in the back, smiling broadly, and Chip and Andrea were in the center section. They looked a little nervous for me, and I was tempted to wink at them to show them I was OK. But the Reverend Mother shouldn't be winking at the audience. Miss Cason would faint.

Maria went to work as a governess for the von Trapp family, and I watched my classmates play the roles of the children, running and scampering. It looked like fun. Before long, however, Maria had fallen in love with Captain von Trapp and, rather than face her feelings, had returned to the convent.

It was my big scene. When the curtain rose, I was at my desk, and the trembling Maria was kneeling in front of me. I stood, asked if she were in love with the captain, and the music from the orchestra started the introduction to my song. I stood at the backlit window and sang, "Climb Ev'ry Mountain."

> Climb ev'ry mountain, search high and low,
> Follow ev'ry byway, ev'ry path you know.
> Climb ev'ry mountain, ford ev'ry stream,
> Follow ev'ry rainbow, till you find your
> dream.
> A dream that will need all the love you can
> give
> Ev'ry day of your life, for as long as you live.
> Climb ev'ry mountain, ford ev'ry stream,
> Follow ev'ry rainbow, till you find your
> dream.

By the last line, I was belting out the song with everything I had. The adrenaline, or whatever it was I felt when I was actually performing, helped me sing better than I ever had in rehearsal. When I finished and looked down at Maria, there was a look in Shalisa's eyes I'd never seen before: respect.

I finished the scene and sat in the wings until the last scene where the nuns hide the von Trapps in the convent and then send them out over the mountains to freedom. With the other nuns, I waved them over the "mountains," which were really plywood steps covered by painted humps, and watched the curtain fall.

It was a good performance, and we had all

done well, but I didn't feel as high after this show as I had when Astronaut Junior High did our performance of the music from *Oklahoma!* Astronaut's production was really skimpy compared to this production, but being in a performance hall and having fancy props and an orchestra didn't matter to me. It was more fun doing a skimpy show with my friends than being in an extravagant production with people who thought I was weird.

After the show, it was a little awkward when Mom and Tom and Dad and Max came backstage to congratulate me. It was the beginning of my weekend with Dad and Max, so Mom and Tom slipped off and said they'd see me later. Dad did extend his hand to Tom, though, and introduced himself. I thought that was a pretty brave gesture.

Chip and Andrea made their way backstage, too, and Dad offered to take us all out for burgers and ice cream, if I'd wash the wrinkles off my face. I did.

It was a great night. We sat in a crowded booth at Bob's Burgers and laughed until we cried. Dad told corny jokes, and Max told us how well Fido's Fricassee was selling, and Chip held my hand, and Andrea whispered secrets in my ear about the kids at school. It felt like old times, and I loved it.

Max and I spent Thanksgiving at the Harris

house. I really felt sorry for Max because there was no where for him to go and nothing for him to do. You've got to understand a kid like Max—boredom is like brain death for him. He looked through the Harrises' library, which held mostly law books that we weren't allowed to touch. Then he checked outside by the pool, but everything was clean and sparkling—no algae growths, no ant beds, no wild life, no termites to trap. Max was totally bored.

There was nothing in Nick's room that interested Max. In fact, Max hardly knew Nick at all and didn't like talking to him much. Nick was sports-crazy, and Max has never been interested in sports. Max wandered into the kitchen, but Uncle Jacob was wrestling with the turkey and told Max to get out of the way. Max wasn't used to Uncle Jacob's gruffness, so he left the room quickly.

Things were really awkward at dinner when Tom Harris tried to make Max feel at home. "Well, Max, how's school?" Tom asked.

"What do you mean?" Max asked, putting down his knife and fork. "Do you mean in the academic, social, or general sense?"

Tom shifted in his chair uneasily. "Uh, in the general sense."

"I suppose it's fine," Max answered, carefully cutting his turkey. "Is there anything more specific you'd like to know?"

Tom massaged his throat nervously. "No, I guess not." He gave Mom a half-grin, and Mom closed her eyes and shook her head. I could guess what she was thinking: *Max is just like his father—impossible to talk to.*

If Tom wasn't going to take an interest in Max, and if Mom was going to write him off because he was like Dad, poor Max would never fit into the Harris part of the family. He'd just be an occasional visitor, and I'd lose my brother nearly altogether.

I ate a forkful of turkey stuffing and tried not to cry.

My fourteenth birthday was a week away, on December 8. Usually I had a big cake with sparklers and candles on it, *anything* but Christmas decorations, but so far this year, no one had mentioned anything about my birthday. There was a big calendar in our kitchen at home, and on my birthday Mom had written "16 days" which meant there were sixteen days until the wedding. That was all she was thinking about.

The days were passing quickly, I had to admit, with school, and packing to move, and real estate people coming through the house all the time with prospective buyers. Christmas was around the corner, too, and Mom had arranged it with Dad that Max and I would go home with him after the wedding on Christmas Eve, so we'd spend Christmas in his condo. Mom would be on her honeymoon, anyway, so she wouldn't even miss us.

I had more people on my Christmas shopping list this year than I'd ever had. One afternoon after school I took a city bus to the mall with my life savings. For Mom, I bought a bottle of perfume. It probably wasn't nearly as nice as the perfumes Tom Harris would buy her, but it was the thought that counted, right?

I found a book on computer programming for Dad and a book on bees for Max. He liked animals, and he used to have an ant farm, so I figured he'd like bees, too.

I bought Chip a sweater that matched his blue eyes. It was soft and downy, and I loved just touching it. He'd like it, I was sure. For Andrea, I found a pair of seashell earrings that would hang down at least three inches in her long, blonde hair. For Uncle Jacob, I found a small leather-covered notebook he could use for making lists or jotting down notes to himself. I even bought a paperweight for Doug Richlett and a rhinestone collar for Suki. Dogs deserve Christmas presents, too.

At the bottom of my list were two names I didn't want to think about, but I knew I had to get them something: Tom and Nick. Nick wasn't so hard to shop for; I just went to the sports department and bought him three pairs of athletic socks. It wasn't a glamorous gift, but hey—stepbrothers aren't glamorous, are they? But what could I get Tom?

I left the big department store and walked slowly through the mall, trying to think of a gift for Tom that wouldn't insult my mother and wouldn't flatter Tom too much. I didn't have much money left, either.

There! At the corner of the mall was a typical tourist trap, one of those "Make Your Own Record" shops where you plunk down ten dollars, pick an accompaniment tape, and sing away. At the end of the "session," they hand you a cassette tape with your own name on the label.

Mom would love it, and if Tom didn't like it, well, he'd have to say he did or he'd insult Mom. I walked in without hesitation. "Do you have 'Climb Ev'ry Mountain?'" I asked the guy behind the desk.

He gave me a strange look, then looked through his list of songs. "Yeah, we do," he said. "We don't get many calls for it, though."

"You're getting one today," I said. I pointed through the doorway that led to the little studio. "I just go in here?"

"Yeah." The guy smiled. "We'll make you a star."

I walked into the room, put down my packages, and shut the door. I put on the head-

phones and adjusted the microphone so that
it pointed to my chin. "You don't have to
make me a star," I said into the mike, so the
guy in the sound booth could hear. "Just make
me a Christmas present."

18

Mom didn't forget my birthday. When I got up for breakfast that morning, there were two small gift-wrapped presents on the kitchen counter. "Happy birthday, Cass," the card on the first package said. "From Mom and Tom."

I opened the box and found a beautiful gold chain inside. It was heavy and probably very expensive. Mom must have picked it out, and Tom probably paid for it, I figured. I put it back in the box and poured my bowl of cereal.

I opened the second package. It was from Dad and Max, and contained a pair of pearl earrings. *Why jewelry?* I wondered. Mom probably told Dad I needed something nice to wear for the wedding. But they were nice gifts, and I was just glad someone remembered my birthday with all the other stuff going on.

It was an ordinary day at school, except that

Shalisa was playing Lady Bountiful by handing out gilt-edged invitations to the McRay Christmas party. Everyone in the ninth-grade class was supposed to get one, but she didn't just hand them out all at once. She picked a special time and place to give each invitation, and by the end of the day I was wondering if I'd get one at all. I didn't really care about going to her stupid party, but I'd feel awful if I was the only kid who didn't get one.

Finally, after dance class, she came my way. "Cassie Perkins," she said, smiling and showing her perfectly white teeth. "We would simply love for you and your family to come. This invitation is for you, your mother, and Tom Harris, of course. He and my parents belong to the same club, you know."

"I know." I sighed and took the invitation. "I don't know if we can make it, though, because everything's getting pretty hectic with the wedding," I said, taking off my dance shoes. "We have a rehearsal, and fittings for our dresses, and meetings with the florist, and . . ."

"I know those things can be a bother," Shalisa said. "But you won't want to miss this. After all, it's your mother's second wedding, but this will be your first McRay Christmas party."

I opened my mouth, but she lightly tapped my arm. "No excuses, Cassie. I will count on your being there."

154

She flitted away toward another group of kids, and I picked up my stuff and left the rehearsal hall. As I passed out of the room, I dropped her invitation in the trash.

I didn't want to spend the night of my birthday alone, so I called Chip. "Do you want to go to church tonight?" he asked. Yes. I wanted to be with friends. He and his family picked me up.

All the usual kids were gathered in the church youth room, and Doug had to bang on a table to get everyone's attention. "It's good to see you all here," he said, smiling. "Who has something they want to share with the group?"

Several kids stood up and shared what they had been learning at school, or how they had been telling their friends about Jesus Christ. I was kind of embarrassed, because I'd never told anyone about Jesus, but I didn't even know how to begin. Then Doug asked if we had anything we wanted the group to pray about.

I raised my hand, and Doug nodded toward me. "Cassie?"

"My mom's getting married on Christmas Eve," I said, deciding to be honest. "And I think it's a big mistake. I want you all to pray that God will stop this marriage so my brother and I won't have our lives ruined." I shrugged. "That's it."

Doug looked down at the floor for a minute,

then he looked back up at me. "Do you really want us to pray that the marriage will be stopped, or would you rather we prayed for God's will in the situation?" he asked gently. "I know it may seem like a mistake to you, but are you willing to trust God and let him work it out?"

I'd heard that somewhere before, but now it made me think. Other kids were waving their hands to give their prayer requests, but Doug put his hand out to keep them quiet. He was looking at me.

"I don't know," I confessed. "I'm trying to trust God, but I don't want my mom to marry this man. I don't want to move. I don't want to have a stepfather."

I realized I sounded very selfish. I was listing all of my wants instead of thinking about what was best for my mom. I bit my lip.

"God knows what you want, and he knows what you need," Doug said. "You can trust him, Cassie, if you will."

"OK," I said, too tired to fight any more. "I'll pray for God's will, and I'll trust him."

After church, Chip asked his dad to drop us off at the corner so he could walk me home. As we walked, he pulled a thin rectangular package out of his jacket pocket. "Happy birthday," he said, looking into my eyes. "I hope you like it."

"I'm sure I will," I said, tearing off the wrapping paper. Inside was a cassette tape of a song, "Trust His Heart."

"Listen to the song tonight," Chip said. "I think you'll really like it. The song really helps me when things aren't going right."

"Thanks, Chip," I said, leaning my head toward his shoulder. "I know I asked God to take control of my life, but I sure feel like I'm messing it up sometimes."

"We all do that sometimes," Chip said, slipping his arm around me.

We walked in quiet for a few minutes until we were at my house. The big For Sale sign hung in the front yard.

"Has anybody bought your house yet?" Chip asked, putting his hands in his pockets. The night was chilly.

"No," I said, shaking my head. "But my dad can't wait until it sells because he won't have to make two house payments any more." I laughed. "I guess there is something good in all this."

Chip nodded. "Things will be OK, Cassie. Maybe there's a lot more good in it than you realize."

"Maybe." I rocked on my heels. "Thanks again for the tape. I guess I should go in before we both freeze."

"OK. Good night."

Before I even knew what happened, Chip grabbed my shoulders, pulled me close, and kissed my forehead. I was so startled I didn't do anything, and it was only as I watched him turn from the driveway onto the sidewalk that I wished I'd turned my face upwards so he could have kissed my lips instead. That was one lousy thing about being short.

But it was still a kiss, and a nice one, too. Andrea would die when I told her! Chip had kissed me! I ran inside to give Andrea a call.

That night I put my new cassette in my Walkman as I lay in bed. The song had a simple melody, but it was the words that got to me:

> All things work for our good,
> Though sometimes we can't see
> How they could.
> Struggles that break our hearts in two
> Sometimes blind us to the truth.
> Our Father knows what's best for us;
> His ways are not our own:
> So when your pathway grows dim
> And you just can't see him,
> Remember—he's still on the throne.
> God is too wise to be mistaken.
> God is too good to be unkind.
> So when you don't understand,
> When you don't see his plan,
> When you can't trace his hand,
> Trust his heart.

Could I trust God's heart? I was trying to.

19

Mom and I finally agreed on our part of the guest list. I wanted to invite Andrea and her parents, but Mom said no. "It's hard, Cass," she explained. "Your father and I used to do everything with Cathy and Ernie Milford. I just don't think they'd want to be here at the wedding."

"But Andrea's my friend."

"But I can't mail an invitation just to Andrea!" Mom was getting frustrated with me. She sighed. "I tell you what. Why don't you have Andrea spend the night with you the night before the wedding. That way she'll be here anyway, and we won't have to send an invitation at all. OK?"

I nodded. If Andrea's parents wouldn't mind her being away the night before Christmas Eve, it would work out fine. But there was another problem. "What about Chip? You said I could invite Chip."

Mom sighed. "I don't even know his parents."

"Then you won't offend them if you just invite Chip."

Mom pushed a blank envelope toward me. "OK, fill it out. Invite him."

Tom's guest list was huge, with probably two hundred names of business associates, friends, and fellow country-clubbers. Plus, since he had been a widower for almost ten years, he could even invite old family members that were relatives of his late wife. Nick was excited about seeing cousins, aunts, and uncles he hadn't seen in a long time.

Our part of the guest list was infinitesimal, as Max would say. Mom had only been divorced a few months, so anyone who knew her as part of "Claire and Glen" wasn't invited. Mom said they would feel too awkward. Dad wasn't invited either, of course, and neither was anyone from his side of the family. I was almost surprised she wanted Max to come, but it was his job to carry the ring on a pillow down the stairs.

Mom had invited a few of her girlfriends from the women's club, and I was allowed (barely) to invite Chip and Andrea. Shalisa and her parents were invited, of course, as part of Tom's guest list. I certainly had nothing to do with that.

Mom asked me again and again what I was going to sing, but I had no idea. I didn't want to sing anything romantic because the idea of romance between my Mom and Tom Harris was crazy. I still felt nauseous whenever he even put his arm around her. I didn't want to sing anything traditional like "I Love You Truly" because that was just too old-fashioned. Mom didn't want any popular songs, though, so I could only think of one thing.

"How about 'Climb Ev'ry Mountain?'" I asked her. "It's nice, it's pretty, and I know it."

Mom thought a minute, her forehead crinkling. "I never would have thought of it," she said.

"A dream that will need all the love you can give," I quoted the words. "I think it fits."

Mom nodded thoughtfully. "OK. 'Climb Ev'ry Mountain' it is."

We had a big rehearsal dinner at the Harris house the night before the wedding. Uncle Jacob, Nick, and Tom were wearing tuxedos, and Andrea walked around with her mouth open the entire night. "Cassie Perkins, I can't believe how lucky you are!" she said, looking over the house and the dining room. "This is like a palace!"

161

I had to admit the place did look nice. Mom had redecorated the main rooms in more up-to-date colors and styles, plus everything was decorated for the wedding and Christmas. There were evergreen boughs tied to the spiral staircase, with elaborate red velvet ribbons dangling among them. A huge Christmas tree, probably twenty feet tall, stretched from the floor to the cathedral ceiling in the living room. There was another tree in the den, and a gaudy outdoor tree festooned with lights out by the pool.

I took Andrea up to my bedroom, although I guessed it wouldn't be officially mine until after the wedding. Mom had ignored my request for black and decorated it in my favorite color, periwinkle blue. My antique furniture was all in place, and there were periwinkle curtains over the big window, with tiny petal-pink bows on everything from the bedspread to the waste-basket.

"This is gorgeous," Andrea said, gasping as she came in. "No wonder you wanted to leave all that other stuff."

"I didn't want to leave it," I said, falling onto my bed. "I had no choice. Mom did this room, and I have to keep it like this."

"Well, you have to admit it's beautiful," Andrea said, plumping the new pink pillow in Suki's tiny bed. She giggled. "And it's a lot better than black."

I laughed. "Yeah, I guess so. Tom wanted to put a Christmas tree in here, too, with pink and blue bows, but I told him not to bother because I'd be at Dad's on Christmas."

"He seems really nice." Andrea was looking out the window at Tom's Mercedes.

I shook my head. "That's because he's not going to be your stepfather. But I don't know that he's going to be mine, either."

"What on earth do you mean?" Andrea stepped back from my window.

"I was praying that they wouldn't get married, but now I'm praying for God's will," I said. "And if it's God's will that they don't get married, then something will happen to stop it, no matter what they've planned." I gave my head a definite nod. "Just wait and see."

Andrea looked around and ran her hand over the soft material of the curtains. "You're crazy, girl, if you try to stop it."

"I'm not going to try," I promised, crossing my heart. "I'm just going to wait and see what happens."

Tonight's party was small compared to the one that would be held after the wedding tomorrow, and there was a lot of laughing and talking. There were eight of us: Tom, Mom, Nick, Uncle Jacob, the Reverend Bob Martin, Andrea, Max, and me.

Max stood quietly during the rehearsal, and

163

he looked uncomfortable in his new dark suit. I felt sorry for him, so I patted him on the shoulder as we stood at the top of the stairs with Mom. "It'll be OK, Whiz Kid," I promised. "Trust me."

Max gave me a doubtful look.

"Cassie, you'll come down the stairs first," Pastor Martin called from the bottom of the stairs. "You'll come down here and sing the song. Then Nick and Tom will come out and stand with you at the bottom of the steps here, and then Max and your mother will come down the stairs." He looked around. "Everybody got it?"

Mom seemed a little nervous. "Cassie, you'll be carrying a basket of roses, and Max, you'll be carrying the pillow, but keep the ring in your pocket, OK?"

Max nodded.

"And please, please," Mom begged, "don't do any experiments with it, OK? You promise you won't melt it or eat it or feed it to something?"

Max rolled his eyes. "Cut it out, Mom."

Mom nodded her head rapidly. "OK." She patted him on the back. "I just want everything to be perfect. All those people will be here!"

For the first time, I wondered if Mom was worried about fitting into Tom's high society world, too. Mom had always been active with her women's club, and she had clients who were well-to-do, so I had never thought that Mom would be nervous about the country-clubbers. But Mom didn't have anything to worry about. She was always perfect.

We walked through the ceremony, and Pastor Martin chuckled. "This is where I would say, 'I pronounce you man and wife,' but if I say that now, we won't need to have a wedding tomorrow, will we?"

Everyone laughed politely at his joke, and Tom turned to the group. "I guess we can eat now. Right, Reverend? Let's adjourn to the dining room."

Andrea gave me another one of her this-is-incredible looks, and I shrugged. Maybe by tomorrow night this would all be over and I'd be back with my normal mom in a normal house and Tom Harris would be out of my life. Maybe.

20

It was a beautiful morning, I had to admit. The sun was shining, the air was cool, and that tingly smell of Christmas was in the air. The wedding was set for two o'clock, and even now, at eight, the people from the rental company were bringing in the two hundred or so white folding chairs that would be placed throughout the living room and foyer.

The florist and the caterer arrived at ten, and the sound of so many voices woke Andrea up. She stirred and looked across at me where I sat by the window. "What time is it?" she croaked.

"It's about ten," I said, looking out the window again. "You wouldn't believe all the commotion downstairs. Uncle Jacob wants us to stay out of the way. If you want, he'll make us a breakfast tray and we can eat in here."

"Breakfast in bed?" Andrea sat up, smiling.

"Honestly, Cassie, this is like a vacation. And you get to live here!"

"It's not always like this," I said, rubbing Suki's belly. Poor old dog, the older she got, the more she slept. "I've got to put Suki out, and I'll bring us breakfast when I come back."

"Is Nick up?" Andrea asked, blushing. "I don't want to go out without my makeup if he's around."

I laughed. "I thought you didn't like him."

"I like him, sure," Andrea said, grinning. "But not as a boyfriend—at least, not yet."

There were decorators out by the pool, where the wedding cake was being set up, in the dining room, where the food was arranged, and in practically every room but the bedrooms. One lady was even in the downstairs bathroom arranging flowers and wedding soaps by the marble sink. "Excuse me," I said, walking in on her.

"Would you please tell the guys doing the chairs to leave an extra aisle toward the powder room?" she asked, not even looking up. "Men have no sense of how to arrange things."

"Uh, OK," I mumbled, backing out. She probably thought I was the maid.

I saw a nice-looking man setting out chairs and jerked my thumb toward the bathroom. "There's a lady in there who says to leave an aisle for the powder room," I told him. "OK?"

"Sure," he said, smiling. He had a nice smile, and for some reason, I felt better.

Uncle Jacob had left us a tray in the kitchen, and because we wouldn't get lunch, there was a lot of food on it. Andrea and I scarfed everything down in my room, watching people come and go from my window.

I saw our dresses arrive at eleven-thirty, and soon after, Mom came in carrying my dress of maroon velveteen and her dress of ivory lace. The dresses were made from the same pattern and suited us both pretty well. Mom's was especially pretty in all that lace. It had a high neck and a lace medallion on the bodice, with an old-fashioned gathering of lace around her hips. Both dresses had pearls on the bodice and sparkled in the sunlight.

"How pretty!" Andrea said, her eyes gleaming. She waited until Mom left, then whispered to me, "I almost wish my mom was getting married again!"

"No, you don't," I said. Suki climbed into my lap, and I hoisted her up so that she could look out the window, too. She was smiling and panting from the excitement of so many people around.

Max knocked on the door and came in. He had spent the night in Nick's room, but he didn't look like he had slept much. "How are you and Nick getting along?" I asked, patting the floor beside me so he'd sit down.

"Not great," he said, sitting Indian-style on the carpet. "We just don't have much in common."

Mom burst into the room, breathless from rushing up the stairs. "Max, there you are," she said. "Is your suitcase packed for your father's tonight? Cass, will you be ready to go after the wedding? I don't know for sure when he's coming to get you two, and I know I won't be able to run around and pack your suitcases."

"Don't worry, Mom," I said. "We'll just slip out with Dad. We'll be ready to go. We'll take Andrea home, too."

Mom looked relieved. "Good. Max, you'd better take a shower and get dressed. The photographer's coming at one, and we're all supposed to be dressed in our wedding clothes for pictures. It's time to get ready!"

I looked up toward the sky. If God was going to do anything to stop this wedding, he'd better do it soon.

At one o'clock sharp, we were all dressed and posed on the stairs for the wedding pictures. Mom and Tom didn't care anything about the old superstition that says the groom shouldn't see the bride on their wedding day, because here they were, posing for pictures as if they were married already. I thought the whole thing was silly, posing with rings and flowers, when they weren't even married yet.

"OK, now let's get an entire family shot," the photographer said, looking around. "Who's family?"

An assortment of people climbed onto the stairs, people I didn't even know. Tom's mother was there, Nick, Uncle Jacob, Max, me, Mom, Tom, Tom's brother Steve and his wife, and a couple of little kids. "Is that everybody?" the photographer asked, when I suddenly remembered. "I want Suki," I said, making a mad dash for the back stairs. "I'll be right back!"

As I ran, I heard Tom say something about stopping me, but Mom said, "I can't stop her, she's already gone." *Ha ha.* Tom was going to have Suki in his family picture whether he wanted her or not.

I was quick, and a couple of minutes later I was posed with all those other people on the stairs. "Hurry up," Mom muttered between her teeth as she tried to smile. "People are beginning to arrive. They can't see us like this."

"Say cheese," the photographer said, and we all did. The camera flashed, and the flash startled Suki. She wriggled out of my arms, scratched me, and I let her go.

"Ouch!" I yelped, looking at my arm. No one else paid any attention because they were trying to untangle themselves and get off the stairs without breaking their necks. I rubbed my arm and went to get Suki, but the front door opened, and she scampered out onto the lawn, eager to greet the people who were arriving.

"Please catch that dumb dog," Tom snapped, losing his temper. I looked up at him without a word and went out the door, but not before I heard Mom say, "Tom, it wasn't her fault. Ease up." They weren't even married, and they were fighting already.

Suki was sitting on the edge of the driveway, smiling at a guy in a uniform who was hired to park cars. He knelt and snapped his fingers. "Here doggie," he called.

"Wait!" I called, but too late. Seeing a new friend, Suki dashed across the driveway just as a big, black Lincoln Continental pulled into the drive. I heard a yelp and saw Suki disappear under the front wheel.

I couldn't move. The car just kept moving, unaware of what had happened, and my ears were filled with a funny roaring noise. The parking guy ran toward me as I ran toward Suki.

"Don't look!" he yelled, grabbing my shoulders and pushing me back. "Get out of here, kid! You don't want to see that."

I was crying, reaching for Suki, and that guy was pushing me back into the house where a group of confused people shook their heads and wondered why the bridesmaid was screaming. Another man in a dark suit walked over and looked down at the driveway. I couldn't see what he was doing, but he took off his coat and laid it over something on the pavement.

That did it. I broke free and ran to the driveway. I lifted off the coat and saw Suki, her eyes as buggy and brown as ever. She was alive.

She whimpered softly, and I knelt there on the pavement, not caring about my dress. I put my face down to hers and rubbed her velvet ears. "I'm sorry, Suki," I whispered, putting my cheek on her face. I felt her little sandpaper tongue lick the tears from my face. Then she was still.

Someone lifted me away, and some woman took my hand and led me upstairs, fussing about dirt on my dress. Andrea was beside me, too, and I didn't know how long she had been there. While the woman unzipped my dress to clean it, I looked out my window and saw Max and Tom standing by the coat on the driveway. Max had his face hidden in his hands, and Tom put his hand on Max's shoulder.

Mom came in then, pale and worried, and she looked out the window, too. We saw Tom rub Max's head, then Tom turned, got in his Mercedes, and drove away.

Mom sat on the edge of my bed, and now she was crying, too.

21

I heard a clock downstairs chime twice, and I knew there were two hundred people waiting for a wedding that might not happen. I was still lying on my bed, in my slip, because a maid was fussing over my dress with a steamer. Mom was sitting in my favorite wing chair, newly-recovered, and her face looked as if it had been carved in wax. There was no color, no emotion.

I was thinking. There was nothing to do but think. I thought about Suki, the horrible suddenness of her death, and about how stupid I had been to bring her downstairs. Was this God's idea of punishing me for trying to make Tom mad, or was it a very unfunny way of calling off the wedding? If this is what it took to call off the marriage, why did Suki have to be the sacrifice?

"Please God," I whispered, "I take it back.

Let them get married. Can you bring Suki back? I'm sorry for everything." But it was too late. Suki wasn't coming back. Max and Nick had picked her up and taken her someplace. They'd probably bury her later. At least there were enough flowers in this house to give her a decent funeral.

Time passed slowly. I could hear the guests getting restless downstairs, but someone must have suggested that the orchestra play to entertain them, so strains of songs like "Silver Bells" and "We've Only Just Begun" began to float up the stairs to us.

When the clock struck three, there was a knock on the door. "Mrs. Perkins?" It was the voice of Pastor Martin. "What should I do, Mrs. Perkins?"

"I don't know," Mom called through the closed door. Her words were slow and precise. "It's not my house, so I don't know what to tell you."

She was suffering, too, I could see it. She had been sitting in that chair, silent and still, for more than an hour. Where had Tom gone? Had the responsibilities of the Perkins family been too much for him? Had I driven him over the edge? Would Mom ever forgive me for making Tom walk away?

Andrea had been sitting on the bed next to me, and she got up to look out the window for

176

about the fortieth time. "Tom's coming," she said, excited. "I see him. Gray Mercedes, right? He just pulled up."

Pastor Martin heard her, and we heard his footsteps go down the stairs. In a few minutes he was back, rapping on our door again. "Ladies, we're ready to begin the ceremony," he said. "Are you dressed?"

"Just a minute," Andrea called. She and the maid practically stood me up and put my dress on me. Andrea wiped my eyes and reapplied blush to my cheeks. "OK."

The door opened, and Pastor Martin and Tom stood outside the door. "Everyone's waiting," Tom said, gently, looking at Mom. "Isn't it about time you became Mrs. Harris?"

Mom stood up slowly and looked at him. "Where have you—," she began, but Tom interrupted.

"I brought your flowers up," he said, handing the bouquet of orchids to Mom. He had my basket of roses at his feet, and he reached down for it. "And for you, Cassie."

I reached out for the basket automatically, my emotions frozen. But something was wrong with the basket, it was too heavy. I gave it a little shake. "What on earth?"

The basket was a hamper-type, with roses and ribbons sticking out from one side. I lifted the cover off the other side, and to my amazement, inside was a tiny pug-nosed puppy.

"For you," Tom said simply. "Because this wouldn't be home without you—and your dog."

I just stared at him while Mom melted into his arms. "I love you, Tom Harris," she said, turning her face toward his. "I truly do."

They went down the stairs arm-in-arm, and I followed them, completely out of our carefully-arranged wedding party order. When we reached the curve of the staircase, the guests began applauding, and Mom's head brushed Tom's shoulder. Max and Nick looked up at me, and Chip was behind them. I smiled and kept my free hand on the soft, warm treasure in my basket of roses.

A new puppy wouldn't take Suki's place—no dog ever could. But maybe this puppy would be a good friend, too. Maybe there was a time and place for starting again.